Sesher Kobita
The Last Poem

Anindita Mukhopadhyay teaches history at University of Hyderabad. She has translated for research purposes over the last few years. She is the author of *Behind the Mask: the Cultural Definition of the Legal Subject in Colonial Bengal 1175-1900*.

Sesher Kobita
The Last Poem

RABINDRANATH TAGORE

Edited and translated by
Anindita Mukhopadhyay

Published by
Rupa Publications India Pvt. Ltd 2006
161-B/4, Gulmohar House,
Yusuf Sarai Community Centre,
New Delhi 110049

Sales centres:
Bengaluru Chennai
Hyderabad Kolkata Mumbai

Translation copyright © Anindita Mukhopadhyay 2006

This is a work of fiction. Names, characters, places and incidents are either the product of the author's imagination or are used fictitiously and any resemblance to any actual person, living or dead, events or locales is entirely coincidental.

All rights reserved.
No part of this publication may be reproduced, transmitted, or stored in a retrieval system, in any form or by any means, electronic, mechanical, photocopying, recording or otherwise, without the prior permission of the publisher.

P-ISBN: 978-81-291-0937-8
E:ISBN: 978-93-5702-060-2

Fourteenth impression 2026

15 14

Printed in India

This book is sold subject to the condition that it shall not, by way of trade or otherwise, be lent, resold, hired out, or otherwise circulated, without the publisher's prior consent, in any form of binding or cover other than that in which it is published.

Contents

Introduction	1
1. Amit's Tale	27
2. The Collision	46
3. Preface	55
4. Labanya's History	61
5. Striking up Acquaintance	71
6. Beyond Introductions	78
7. Matchmaking	93
8. Labanya's Debate	113
9. Change of Residence	120
10. The Second Sadhana	128
11. The Theory of Union	136
12. The Last Evening	146

13. Apprehension . . . 159
14. Dhumketu or Haley's Comet . . . 171
15. Hindrance . . . 181
16. Freedom . . . 195
17. The Final Ode . . . 200
    Select Bibliography . . . 212

Introduction:

Anindita Mukhopadhyay

PART I

How does a novel, with a title like *Sesher Kobita – The Last Poem*, enter the reader's world? Novels and poetry are surely different genres of literature. The answer lies in the way Tagore unfolds his characters, ambidextrously using both genres to produce a distinctive, lyrical prose. His characters in *The Last Poem* are introduced with a certain purpose. Tagore removes all the props – social conventions, society, even family – just to set a man and a woman talking to one another. Tagore gives us Amit Rai and Labanyalata, introduced to the reader through the voice of a young and unknown author. This author remains anonymous throughout the text. In fact, apart from a few pages, where his racy observations sketch in Amit, his set and his sisters, he unobtrusively retreats from the position of the narrator. But, in this cameo role, he does not waste any time in catapulting Amit Rai straight into the novel using fast-paced and satirical prose. He seems to delight in hurling other characters into the novel as well: Labanya at the beginning of the novel and Katy/Ketoki at the near end, hit the reader like projectiles, so sudden are their appearances. The sharp foxtrot on artificial Western mannerisms and orthodoxies embeds the characters in a society undergoing deep cultural changes at various levels. The Inga-Bangiya upper class, fiercely Western, carefully avoided anything 'Bengali'. Though the young narrator's attitude is breezily nonchalant as he describes Amit's sisters and friends, the bite is unmistakable (p.33). His sardonic eye notes the fashionable female apparel and the extravagances of brand-new society manners, and flashes across to observe male affectations with equal mockery (pp.172-175). The other extreme – social orthodoxy – is not held up as the ideal solution for the retention and development of strong cultural roots either. Here, too, the young narrator is at his cynical best as he lightly touches upon obsolete social and religious customs that physically and mentally shackle women (pp.57-58).

Labanya's father, the hybrid intellectual, supplied the middle path to a balanced cultural language of self-growth. But there is a hint of criticism here as well – for Labanya, the much-loved, self-sufficient, intellectual daughter, had forgotten, or was made to forget, the feminine language of tenderness and understanding (pp.62-63).

Rabindranath, exploring various alternatives for the self-evolution of young men and women, carefully lays bare the emotional emptiness that individuals, caught in social transitions, might have possibly experienced. His solution to the rudderless existence of both men and women, trapped into moving back and forth meaninglessly on the same groove, is quietly rebellious – dialogue between the two sexes. *The Last Poem* is about a reaching out of conversational tentacles to feel the presence of the sexual Other, shorn of the weight of social conventions that only allow the parroting of meaningless phrases at the tea-table – where there is no true communication, where personalities simply hide behind the empty mask of manners.

An intelligent young man like Amit is dissatisfied with the life of a showpiece in a showcase, but it is a role he can perform to perfection. Subtly, Tagore implies that behind Amit's cultivated unconventional appearance and sharp intellect lies a deep psychological lack, which his social set, blinded by its own glitter, cannot fathom. There is a hint here of only the power of provocative speech and youth which bestows on Amit a certain presence – otherwise he is insubstantial. Certainly Amit flamboyantly exhibits a much-touted general attraction towards the opposite sex, implying that no single woman can capture his erratic fancy. But it is equally true that women, too, skate over him as on a polished surface. They don't take him seriously either. He is a will-o-the-wisp, deliberately placing himself in the margins as an observer, and accepted as such. Even his aggressively masculine identity, which daringly takes on Tagore's 'effeminate' poetry against a loyal audience, remains a series of flamboyant verbal posturings, more for effect than anything else. An old man past his poetic prime, mumbling about tyaga, about pain, is scorned by a crisp young male voice, extolling an aggressive masculinity (p.40).

But Amit's identity is only through words. And words can be spoken only in company, before an audience. He appears to the others as occupying centre-stage, but actually he himself needs the ears and the verbal responses of others – outraged or admiring – to feel reassured about his own 'unique' personality. His sister, Sissy, puts her finger on Amit's ephemeral personality – *Ami, you will spend your life with reflections.* (p.45). His ill-chosen hilly retreat with no company makes his holiday sojourn unutterably dreary. Amit is claustrophobically shut up within himself – and his vast, silent surroundings cannot release him from this prison (p.47). His constant search for mental highs, without which he lapses into somnolence, indicates the hollowness of his assumed masculinity, the artifice of his fake eccentricity. Deep down, Amit is restless for he knows himself to be unreal and incomplete; something vital is absent from his world, and more importantly, from within himself.

A deep, lovely, yet unobtrusive feminine appearance suddenly swings Amit around, making him aware of the reason for his own incompleteness. This is Labanya – herself emotionally suspended in limbo. Her father had taught her to value a cerebral detachment, had trained her intellect diligently through the new educational system that allowed women to compete openly with men. His high pride in her intellectual attainments and the weight of his expectations had turned Labanya away from her deeply feminine nature, while her trained, logically coherent mind had become masculine in its contempt for human weakness. She considered her bashful and inarticulate worshipper, Shobhanlal, who had committed the unpardonable crime of remaining ahead of her in the competitive arena of examinations and marks, a weakling. She rejected him without compunction. Her father committed the error of falling in love, and she repudiated his attempt to support her financially. Labanya, before her motor car fatefully collided with Amit's on the mountain-path, was an independent young woman, rational and impatient of emotional excesses (p.68).

Tagore predominantly uses these two protagonists' voices and conversations to ruminate about possible answers to the problems that a society in flux had thrown up. The young narrator's astute observations and withering wit give way to a graver tone. Questions that *Manusamhita* did not even consider, surface disturbingly here. Marriage is not the dominion of man over woman, but a bond of friendship. Kalidasa sonorously pronounces, from the depths of the emotional history of India, the cultural space for friendship, love and companionship within wedlock: '*Grihini sachiva sakhimithah, Priyashishya lalite kalabidhau* (Wife, minister, friend, favourite disciple in the pursuit of the arts)' (p.137). Amit and Labanya are both ardent readers, and expert navigators of each other's mindscapes. They are friends *and* lovers – there *is* no dividing line. He is Mita (friend) and she is Bonya (tidal wave). This tight emotional and intellectual reciprocity where the lines of communication are like high voltage wires, is to be sustained in marriage: is it possible? Amit, the masculine voice which knows no feminine misgivings, has no doubts at all: it is very possible because he will make it so. Labanya, now with feminine wisdom regained, is an unwilling realist and is painfully aware that the mundane everydayness of married life *would* obtrude into the realms of the mind.

Labanya needled Amit a bit, 'The southern breeze will presumably blow over your terrace as well, but will your new bride always remain new?'

Amit immediately smashed his fist on the table, yelling, 'Always, always, always!!' (p.145).

These are deep waters. Labanya, Tagore's feminine self, understands marriage to be the total acceptance of the partner, complete with warts. She is also aware that Amit has a romantic and worshipful idea of a Labanya who is *his* creation. She is too self-aware to not know that she cannot, she will not accept a fate that condemns her to live within the straitjacket of someone else's desires. Sooner or later such a false existence would become unsustainable: she could not live a lie for ever, even if she was willing to do so. Amit's illusion is bound to crack when thrust into close marital bondage with her physical, embodied presence, a tie which would slam shut all escape routes, and compel a realistic realignment of all his romantic notions about his partner (pp.115-116).

Though Tagore followed a conventionally patriarchal purusa/prakriti divide when it came to questions of masculinity and femininity, even in *The Last Poem*, a work he wrote in 1929 when in his seventies, he was at his most sceptical when it came to the question of the 'sacred' bond of marriage between men and women. In *The Last Poem* he is openly critical of the institution. Labanya's strong opinions, deflecting Yogamaya's own perception of marriage, reflect Tagore's obvious unease with the kind of mental violence that marriage unleashed on unprepared human beings: *It has repeatedly occurred to me, ... that love becomes a tragedy when human beings ... have forcibly wanted to graft their own desires onto someone else. (pp.114-5)*

Yogamaya's defense for marriage is by no means conventional as she is herself a reflective and intelligent woman, wary of social fetters. Possibly her own experiences give her answer a breadth of vision that a woman of lesser intellect would be incapable of putting forward: *when two youngsters desire to settle down, each has to creatively remould the other to a certain extent ... Where there is love, this ... is easy. Where there is none, and a hammer takes its place, what you call 'tragedy' is sure to occur. (p.115)*

Labanya's acidic dismissal of the conventional expectations of the average young men and women, shows disdain of social rules that are governed by the iron rule of averages. She deliberately picks up the exceptional category – to which Amit belongs. She does not include herself in this category, for she has the honesty to acknowledge that she would like nothing better than to be married to Amit. The source of her reluctance to marry Amit is Amit himself. How would Amit reconcile his imaginary Labanya and the requirements of domesticity? The standardised rituals of wedded bliss stand no chance in Amit's imagination, as Labanya knows. Foreshadowing contemporaneous social attitudes, Labanya passes judgment on popular romantic ideas on marital relationships – *I firmly believe that what we consider normally as 'getting', is nothing more than a hand acquiring a hand-cuff.* (p.115)

Tagore was convinced that the older codes for ensuring matrimonial bliss were no longer valid. Marriage, interpreted exactly as a pre-colonial society had understood and experienced it, led in many cases to the asphyxiation of personalities in a changed societal environment. Young women suffered intense mental torment under traditional social conventions. Many of Tagore's short stories and novels certainly mirrored his own intense perturbation over the degree of human suffering. *Yogayog* (Connections) agonised over the fate of Kumudini, tied to Madhusudhan, for whose crude personality she felt no affinity. Kumudini's tortured mind had found no relief even when the novel ended: a relentless female biology compelled her to go back to her husband, whom she had left, for by then she was pregnant. She had to leave her only refuge – her brother, the sole being who was akin to her, and return to an environment where nothing gave her joy.

To this totally undesirable fallout of unsuitable marriages was juxtaposed another breed of young women, numerically very small, but capable of shaking the very foundations of orthodox society. This breed stepped forward when the Swadeshi movement, sweeping thorough Bengal in 1905, demanded the return of indigenous goods in the Indian markets, among other things. But what gave this political movement a totally different spin was the elevation of womanhood to the level of Shakti – the tremendous female energy that galvanised the masculine godhead to action. The women of the antahpura were the source of energy – their intuitive cleaving to the strong ideals of masculinity enthused brave and reckless young nationalists to readily sacrifice their lives for the 'Motherland'.

Tagore, in many of his novels and short stories dwelt on the impact such a heady emotional cocktail had on both young men and women, but especially on women, for they turned away from their femininity and womanliness in the intoxicating spell of being in the public limelight. Ela in *Chaar Adhaay* (Four Chapters), is a typical representative. Ela, convinced along with her revolutionary mentor, that marriage would put a stop to her role as the emblem of feminine strength, and constrict her space solely within the home, thrusts away her own desires. Because of Ela's own blindness to her innate feminine strength, she and Atin are doomed figures. So is Bimala, with her mild mannered husband, Nikhilesh, in *Ghare Baire* (The Home and the World). It is the magnetic pull of a public role that prevents Bimala from recognising her husband's true strength. Sandeep, exuding raw power and masculine aggression in his resolve to free the Motherland, sways and seduces her mind and heart. Bimala's lack of perception of the importance of her true sphere of influence – the home – brings tragedy of catastrophic proportions to many lives, including her own. Masculinity, she learns too late, is not an empty rhetoric that demands that women perform the public role of Shakti to rouse masculine strength and determination for independence. Instead, it is a steadfast adherence to duty and responsibility, with full awareness that such a course could be life-threatening. For Bimala, a different brand of masculinity, stamped with a calm and unshaken resolve, was revealed when the gentle Nikhilesh, without a moment's hesitation, went to stop a communal riot, the inevitable spin-off from Sandeep's misguided Swadeshi politics. Bimala's realisation possibly came too late, as the novel's bitter end indicated, for Nikhilesh was brought back seriously injured, and though his condition was not explicitly stated, he was perhaps beyond all medical aid.

Tagore repeatedly comes back to the main theme consistently pursued through a fair number of novels: that however rational a woman's mind, and however clear her intelligence, she moves away from her true nature if she lacks feminine intuition and wisdom. He creates Labanya initially in the same mould, and highlights her pride in her competitive spirit, and also underscores her emotional barrenness. What releases her from her servitude to her intellect is her deep love for Amit. When she breaks out of the protective intellectual shell and finds her own true feminine nature, she registers her self-transformation with thankful tears (p.118).

Tagore, with acute perception, suggests that the alternatives present within the conventional social and emotional boundaries – liberal or otherwise – produce incomplete individuals. The supposedly traditional set of roles is either a misfit, or is rejected, while new modes of thinking about fundamental social relationships have many detractors. Individualistic young adults fall casualties to these indistinct traces that hint at the realisation of emotional possibilities, yet prove to be strangely elusive at the level of practical reality. Before Amit and Labanya meet by chance through an accident and are instantly drawn to each other, both of them, though young adults, lived in some kind of emotional vacuum. Amit had erected a wall of words around his inner emptiness, hiding behind the veil of his sharp wit, while Labanya, grave, introspective, shunning intimate human contact, a teacher to Surama, Yogamaya Devi's daughter, just locked away her emptiness in her heart, successfully looking away from this dark abyss. Yogamaya Devi, though her employer, is also her loving guardian, and Labanya therefore can project a superficial appearance of serenity and wholeness, an aura which instantly drows Amit to her.

Throughout the novel, Yogamaya Devi is a steady reference point, intellectually alive, yet extremely maternal, providing both the protagonists with a loving buffer on their emotional journey. Amit discovers maternal tenderness, Labanya receives feminine wisdom. Yogamaya Devi's personality had absorbed the turbulent social changes in Bengal. Her world initially had been free because of a liberal father, then chained by an orthodox husband and the requirements of the almanac. Such swings of fortune did not make her intolerant, but unconventionally liberal, where she defines marriage as a union of minds, not bodies. It is really her attitude that quietly allows the romance of Amit and Labanya to progress along the lines that it does. Both Amit and Labanya suddenly grow to maturity under her gentle, yet watchful eye.

For Amit, Labanya's grave and beautiful face, her equanimity in the face of imminent death, her reasonableness, fire his imagination in an instant: whatever was wanting is supplied by the manner of their meeting. Amit thinks exultingly, *My mind tells me, maybe our paired movement has begun.* (p.53). Poetry begins to leak from Amit's soul without end as he seeks inspiration from his secret alter ego, Nibaran Chakraborty, the robust, masculine poet whom Amit produces when occasions demand the necessity of sharp language for which Amit would not be held responsible. Amit, since the moment of meeting Labanya, is joyously transported to an exalted mental level from which vantage point he can see himself more clearly.

Labanya herself realises that the stranger has awakened her supine inner self, and fused her past and present together. Suddenly the long-dammed up pain that her educational training had anaesthetised her against, rushes in. Tagore considers this meeting of Labanya's masculine self with the forgotten feminine one — with its tears and aching emptiness — as the flash-point of a woman's maturity: a lightning-fast recognition of her true nature (p.70). Tagore uses the voice of a mature, wise woman, Yogamaya, to reaffirm this understanding that pain is a woman's constant companion, which no amount of reading will wish away (p.117).

Tagore seems to be holding out a mental ardhanarishwar conjured up from his own imagination, with a woman's form and emotions, yet endowed with an intellect he assumes to be a masculine attribute, to bridge the cognitive gap between men and women. Labanya is always a jump ahead of Amit. Amit, in love with Labanya, acquires depth into his own self – he is in love with himself for having fallen in love with Labanya. He understands his own lack, and that is more than enough for him (pp. 132-133).

He is now a joyous adolescent, instead of a lost one. It has a half-alarming, half-humorous consequence, for even in normal conditions Amit can talk the hind leg off a donkey, but armed with this new-found joy, he is inextinguishable, and yet humorously aware of his insanely voluble, moon-struck self (p.134).

Labanya's cerebral ability to fathom Amit's exuberantly creative masculinity, his personality that will always hunger for the new, and discard the old and the stale, is swift and sure. She engages with him, and Amit suddenly catches hold of his self, the self that had so far evaded him. Labanya, with the depth of her womanly intuition, has not just come to terms with her feminine self, but has also understood Amit inside out. Her mature insights have the power to stun Amit (p.106).

Even his secret poetic self, Nibaran Chakraborty, the weapon he wields to silence a hostile audience, and uses before Labanya to play a lover's game of hide and seek, is obvious to her from the very first. She looks on indulgently while Amit spews words, poems and whims, playfully entering some of the games, but always calling them to a stop when reality intrudes. We see her wistfully ending the world of make-believe – *You desire so many things from me, but I can't imagine how I can even give you a fraction of what you want.*(p.105)

Labanya is also a far cry from stereotypical feminine subservience and can sharply stop Amit from escaping into his own dreamworld when situations get out of hand (p.163). In Labanya, Tagore created his feminine alter-ego – a mythical woman who can enter into the recesses of a man's unconscious because she is intellectually a man. Tagore is like a ventriloquist – now speaking in Amit's voice, now in Labanya's – now as a man, now as a woman, seeking the outer limits of his different selves through their voices. She is clearly androgynous, where her masculine intellect helps her establish contact with her own feminine consciousness, and understand that duty and the nurture of one man, not a public role, was her rightful space in this world. This is Tagore's move away from the Brahminical position on the intellectual inferiority of women: he emphasises that a clear intellect empowers a woman to independently come to a conclusion about her own important 'work' as seva. *The Last Poem* – which ends with Labanya's last poem as the last words of the novel – affirms this in a cerebral celebration of a woman who has finally found herself.

Labanya turns away from the love and friendship that only fed on their minds, considering them to be an insufficient base for marriage. Her awakening to a new self makes the previous self, that had loved Amit deeply, totally redundant, and so she renounces all claims of that self to Amit. In Labanya's mind love and friendship are merely steps to the realisation of the duty and responsibility of the woman. She submits wholeheartedly to the claims that life makes on women. Tagore does not leave a secret mental space for Labanya where she can steal away — he is confident that her reinvented self will not even *desire* it. She deliberately opts for the tender understanding and the forgiveness that Shobhanlal stands for, whose gentle patience can wait an eternity for an answer, for a response, even after a series of cruel rejections from the woman he loves. Tagore, hunting for the perfect woman, finally encounters her in Labanya. She is the perfect balance between the keen mind and cerebral consciousness of a woman's sphere of work or karma, which she proudly declares to be her universe — *I've work, I hold in my hand the whole world* (p.210). The future trajectory of Labanya's life is mapped out: she will be the anchor, the guiding inspiration for a rising career of an academician. Shobhanlal's fantasies about 'Labanya's observations on some of his conclusions based on hard research' (pp.67-68), will all turn real.

Amit, on the other hand, does not find a centre. Tagore's understanding of masculinity is not rooted primarily in any physiological difference between men and women. Masculinity is tortured by the need to create, to discard what has been created and move forever onwards on a quest for the new. Labanya, a man's vision of the perfect feminine self, understands this mad rhythm of masculine creativity: to shackle it will be to strangle it (p.107). Amit will be safer with a woman who is not endowed with the intellectual perception of Labanya, the half male. Labanya, because she is akin to Amit, will be able to see through Amit's physical presence to his mental withdrawal: and her female half will be tormented with this absence (p.109).

This is precisely why Tagore juxtaposes Katy Mitter against Labanya. It is not just a ploy to place Labanya's authentic self against Katy's artificial one, but a deeper intent to demonstrate that *what we consider normally as 'getting', is nothing more than a hand acquiring a hand-cuff (p.115).'* Katy is an average woman, despite her advantages of beauty, wealth and social status. She is incapable of comprehending that a seven-year old relationship, with no mental ability on her side to keep a volatile mind like Amit's engaged, has cost her his real absence. Her average intellect deals with the tangible and the visible. And so, paradoxically, she always hankers after the mere shadow of the man, never the real one. Amit's development, after he is exposed to Labanya, is only towards achieving a degree of tolerance for the real world, as represented by Katy. Before he met Labanya, he had hidden from it under the shield of his intellect. He had ever been the supreme escapist, preferring always to be in the margins – the permanent observer. Labanya gently forces him to confront and accept the constraints of the material world and participate in it as an active agent – and

INTRODUCTION 17

marriage is integral to this reality. Katy literally *is* Amit's hand-cuff! But it is a hand-cuff he can now wear, for Labanya's perspicacity has taught him to function at two levels — in the world of reality, where he can sustain a relationship with Katy, and in the world of fantasy, where he will always have a relationship with Labanya. But even while negotiating the tangible world, Amit does not submit to his fate completely. He defiantly sets about remoulding Katy Mitter, whose anglicised tongue had distorted his name to Amitt Raaye, into Ketoki, and therefore into a more bearable *Bengali* hand-cuff! The analogy Amit gives to describe this negotiation is crude: subconsciously betraying his own distaste for the utilitarian function of marriage — *My relation to Ketoki is definitely love — but it's like water in a pitcher — for everyday use'* (p.206). Amit is triumphantly announcing his ability to cope with the mundane, and revelling in his secret freedom which only Labanya will understand — *I'm the paramahansa of romance ... Victory to my Labanya, victory to my Ketoki, and glory to Amit Rai under all conditions! (p.205)*

Amit Rai still manages to escape, in the end! One wonders, is this secret escapist also Tagore?

The Last Poem is, in the final count, about gaining wisdom and maturity, and accepting the human condition. A reader may argue about gender prejudices and stereotypical notions about men and women, or even elite preoccupations about space, but one cannot set aside such a meaningful engagement with the difficult negotiations all human beings have to make with a life that is inescapably constructed by social and cultural norms.

PART II

The translator, primarily a reader, mediates between the author and his language. An example of such individualistic readings can be Krishna Kripalani's translation of *The Last Poem* – he did not translate the novel's title *Sesher Kobita* at all – he *renamed* it *Farewell, My Friend*. In this sense all translations are battlefields, where struggles with words and their meanings take place between the original text, the translator as the reader *and* the interpreter, and finally the reader reading the translated text. A translation is inevitably an interpretation. *Sesher Kobita* or *The Last Poem*, in the original Bengali, has two distinguishable tempos. The young unnamed author's narration remains on the surface – racy and witty. When Tagore the author takes over, the tone deepens, though flashes of humour lighten the narrative. *The Last Poem* has a specific socio-cultural context which Tagore's inflected Bengali slips in: it is not necessary for him to render them in words. It is very difficult, if not impossible, to capture these unspoken nuances in translations, and *The Last Poem* is no exception. An illustration of this difficulty is seen in the various forms of address – where cultural definitions of relationships are hidden inside words. Ma (mother), Mashi (maternal aunt), Baba (father), Bhai (younger brother), Boudi (sister-in-law), are all words with various layers of meaning, very covertly manifested; though at first glance they only indicate familial relationships. Older men and women fondly call younger women Ma, and the same affection is reflected in Baba when young men are so addressed. Young women call each other Bhai as though it is a gender neutral term, while between young men it reflects male bonding. Mashi is used indiscriminately by young strangers, in order to claim maternal affection as a cultural right. People, men and women, but especially young men, alien to the family, can gain admittance within the tight family unit which includes young married women. This is done by calling them Boudi, which turns them instantly into the wives of hypothetical elder brothers, and therefore sacrosanct. This form of address thus diffuses any threat of sexual transgressions the stranger might represent. These are cultural devices to include any unfamiliar presence into the kinship network and integrate the Outsider immediately within familiar cultural roles. The unfortunate translator, while translating, finds it impossible to capture such rapid shortening of cultural distances where instant cultural fields of inter-personal bonds are evoked with a form of address.

The situation can get even more complex: a young man is attracted to a young woman, yet there is no corresponding form of address within the Bengali culture equivalent to 'Miss Dutt', a colonial mannerism that Amit refuses point-blank to adopt. Unfortunately, indigenous cultural norms do not permit an outright calling out of a name, thereby inducing cultural distances between marriageable young men and women. Even the cheeky Amit views with trepidation such an unforgivable familiarity and can only comically request Labanya to not move beyond hail, as it places him in the most awkward position: *Even if you roar out 'Durga, Durga' at the top of your voice,*

Dasabhuja is not displeased. The problem arises with you ladies.
(p.81)

The difficulties of translation – especially where cultural meanings are expressed through a nuanced prose – have been addressed by many scholars. Tagore himself was aware of stilted sentences and frozen prose when the English language tried to grapple with Bengali inflections. I have therefore retained some Bengali terms in the text, just to retain traces of the original novel. Moreover, Tagore moves the entire story forward with conversations. As the protagonists get into increasingly deeper dialogues with each other, the narrative quickens. But Tagore had launched straightaway into dialogues, with almost no indicators as to the emotional keys registering the flux and change in the voices speaking in the text. It is almost as if he assumes that the Bengali reader will inflect the words to give them their full meaning. At the risk of over-translation and over-interpretation, I have ascribed moods to catch these inflections in conversations. For instance, a typical conversation between Labanya and Amit runs in the original Bengali thus:

'Your statement belongs to a previous age. … let me tell you that my name is not "Amit babu" as far as you are concerned'.

'Perhaps you prefer the English style? Mr. Roy?'

I have tried to convey the light mood of the dialogue – *Amit dodged the logic adroitly, 'Your statement belongs to a previous age... let me tell you that my name is not "Amit babu" as far as you are concerned'. Labanya spiritedly entered into Amit's playful banter, 'Perhaps you prefer the English style? Mr. Roy?'* (p. 75)

Such liberties with the text, to avoid a flat rendition of 'He saids' and 'She saids', is mediating between the possible intent of the author and the translator responding as a reader. But perhaps, in *The Last Poem*, the translator does feel a little emboldened to interpret the text as an individual reader. For the surface of the text contains a story, while the underside of the text explores a layered readers' world. It is almost as though Tagore is peering over his readers' shoulders to see how they are reading him. Tagore produces various voices reading him: the generality read him in blind worship, a few sensitively, while there are rare others who read him critically. In *The Last Poem* Rabindranath tries to assess Tagore, the author wrapped in foggy adulation, through a mercilessly critical reader, Amit. Tagore almost gleefully attacks 'Robi Thakur' as a canon of Bengali literature, wielding Amit like a mace (pp. 43-44).

Amit's exasperation with Tagore's uncritical, worshipful army of admirers has a trace of Rabindranath's own possible disenchantment with his vociferous band of faithfuls. He summons his own secret voice in public – Nibaran Chakraborty – with a naughty play on meanings, for 'Nibaran' literally means 'cannot be stopped' while 'Chakraborty' indicates a person armed with a 'discus' – to challenge Tagore's cult status. Amit's protégé is as unknown as Tagore is known, he ostentatiously displays a 'masculine' aggression, as opposed to Tagore's gentle, 'feminine' lyrics. While everybody reads Tagore, nobody reads Nibaran. Tagore effortlessly dominates the centre stage even while physically absent from literary gatherings, while Amit produces the disembodied voice of Nibaran Chakraborty, present only inside 'a slim canvas-bound note-book' (p.42).

Labanya, an avid reader of Tagore, constantly weaves in 'Robi Thakur' in her conversations. Without aggression, she claims her right to independent judgment against the outright condemnation of 'Robi Thakur' that the critical reader, Amit, advances (pp.89,91). But she can also appreciate Nibaran Chakraborty, the poet whom nobody can access through a published book. Only those Amit considers privileged enough can command Nibaran Chakraborty to give a performance, and Labanya does so with great élan, much to Amit's elation (p.62).

Tagore sets up Labanya as an intelligent reader of Tagore, who can hold Tagore's banner high, and also her own position, yet can make space for other tastes and opinions. Amit's defiant brandishing of Nibaran Chakraborty to counter Tagore only has the effect of earning her delighted approval. Tagore seems to be pushing for an idyllic communion between the consciousness of the reader and that of the author. Even Shobhanlal, the self-effacing and voiceless lover, is another sensitive reader of Tagore. He presents the unpublished poems of Tagore he had received as a gift from Tagore himself, as his personal voice to Labanya.

Labanya recites from these unpublished works of Rabindranath, again as a reader of Tagore's poems that carry the mute Shobhanlal's plea for love and understanding. Both Tagore and Nibaran Chakraborty write for Labanya exclusively. Though they represent two opposite poles, there is a secret point of intersection – Labanya. She, in fact, absorbs the longings wafting from the margins, represented by Shobhanlal and Nibaran Chakraborty, while she faces the dashing Amit squarely, with complete conviction in her own literary taste. Amit violently disagrees with Tagore, yet he has to listen to Labanya reciting Rabindranath's poems, and is, despite his unwillingness, drawn to Tagore's poetry (p.149).

In a foreshadowing of Roland Barthes' *Roland Barthes on Roland Barthes*, Tagore seems to be writing from the liminal position of author and reader. While apparently removing himself from the text, Tagore actually permeates the text at various layers. From a dramatic self-effacement from the world of the critical reader, Amit, Tagore allows himself to be claimed by Amit as well. Amit, shorn of Nibaran Chakraborty's comfortable marginality, loses his nerve as Amit the poet, and helplessly resorts to Tagore – *The wretched Nibaran Chakraborty died as soon as he was found out. So I turn to your poet for my last words to you, no help for it.* (p.206).

As Amit loses his voice, Labanya speaks through her 'last' poem, stamping the moment of the separation of selves – one self realised through love that she gifts to Amit, and the new self which is moving towards the unknown future – as authentically hers, a moment which comes from the node where Nibaran Chakraborty and Rabindranath Tagore meet.

The Last Poem, as a complexly layered novel, is nested within Tagore's understanding that ordinary language is already multi-dimensional, where meaning fractures according to the way individual human beings interpret words according to specific contexts. The scintillating conversation Amit has with Jyotishankar, Yogamaya's son and Amit's willing pupil, shows Tagore pushing meanings beyond dictionary definitions: *Look Jyoti, nothing is plain and simple where human beings are concerned. The dictionary fixes a meaning, but as it interacts with a human variable, the meaning splits in seven different ways, like the Ganga branching off as it nears the sea.* (p.202)

As Tagore taps around the reader's world, he also problematises human communication itself. Words and their meanings do not fit idiosyncratic human needs: the meanings formally attached to words lose their sharp-edged clarity when faced with the fuzziness of human experience.

Jyoti said gropingly, 'You mean to say that marriage does not mean marriage?'

Amit expanded his cryptic statement a little more, 'I'm saying that marriage has a thousand meanings – which blend with different human variables to acquire specific meanings. It is perplexing to try and fix its meaning without the human element.' (p.202)

Despite this inelastic and unreflexive limitation of language, it is still necessary to have language, and to force it to perform at various levels which would in turn connect to different human experiences. Even at its most utilitarian level, it is unsatisfactorily incomplete. Still it remains a means of communication, but one which leaves many gaps at the level of interpretation.

'Why don't you give me your specific meaning,' Jyoti besought Amit, keen to chase away the intellectual fog around this word.

'I cannot define it, explanations will have to come from life. If I say its root word is love, then I go off at a tangent into another word. Because love is even more dynamic than marriage, as far as words and their meanings go'. (p.202-3)

Tagore, via Amit, is positing a chaotic language-field, where meanings have to be chased. Self-evident meanings are deceptive and are capable of distorting human experiences. But ordinary users of language, like Jyoti, are unaware that their habitual linking of only one set of meaning to one word, sharply circumscribes the dynamic potential of the language as a means of communication.

'Then Amitda, we have to stop speaking altogether! If we have to heft a word across our shoulders and chase the meaning, while the meaning dodges left and right as we run after it in hot pursuit, all communication will just stop!' Jyoti was pardonably exasperated. (p.203)

Constant dialogue about what is being left out in interpretation would keep opening fresh lingual chasms. Only conversations could open out the limitless and dynamic possibilities of language, which, when written down formally, always has the effect of freezing their meaning.

Amit became the patronising older man approving of a promising youngster, 'That's not bad, brother!... Communication must somehow go on, and so words are necessary. Some words we deliberately clip when we pull them into market-use, for the reality they contain cannot be expressed in words — so the words remain, but shorn of meaning. Nothing to be done! We just shut our eyes and somehow get on with communication.' (p.203)

Rabindranath is actually suggesting that the language of daily use can function either as very complex sets of signs and signifiers: or it can be deliberately scissored and made to convey only a limited range of meanings. *The Last Poem* reveals Rabindranath playing elaborate games with the fluidity of language, with consummate artistry, under the cover of an unusual love-story.

Chapter 1
Amit's Tale

Amit Rai is a barrister. When the surname 'Rai' metamorphosed into 'Roy' and 'Ray' at the insistence of the English language, what it lost in elegance it gained in variety. To keep its uniqueness intact, Amit endowed it with a novel spelling. So novel was it that Amit's numerous English friends – both male and female – turned it into 'Amitt Raaye'.

Amit's father had been an all-conquering barrister. The enormous wealth he had left behind was enough for the moral degeneration of the next three generations. But Amit, despite the cataclysmic conflict potentially present in his patrimony, had managed to stay on course.

Before he had even registered for the undergraduate programme at Calcutta University, he was packed off to Oxford.

There seven years flew by – taking and not taking exams. Highly intelligent, he had got by without much study, yet one would be hard put to spot any lack in the ultimate product. His father had no high expectations from him. He had merely wished his son to acquire the true-blue Oxonian stamp, which would remain indelible even under the debilitating distractions of various indigenous influences.

I like Amit. Excellent chap. I'm a young writer. My readers' circle is limited, and Amit easily tops my readers' list. The flash and glitter of my literary style has really caught his fancy. He holds that those foremost in fame in our country's literary market cannot lay claim to style. Like the camel, with its uncoordinated, awkward gait and uncouth proportions, plodding its way through desert wastelands, our litterateurs exhibit similar traits while wandering through wordy wastelands. Here I hasten to put in a timely, personal interjection for any critic – this is not *my* opinion.

For Amit, 'fashion' is a mask. An expressive face flares with 'style'. He hardly insists that the lords of literature, writing to please only themselves, have cornered style. Those who write to tickle the palate of others, are mere slaves to fashion's dictates. Bankimchandra's[1] *Bishabriksha* blazes with the highly original 'Bankimi' style. Nasiram's *Monomohaner Mohanbaganey* is just

---

[1] Bankimchandra Chattopadhyay (1838-1894), Bengali novelist whose novels firmly established prose as a literary vehicle for the Bengali language.

a copy cat version – he has totally succeeded in deadening Bankim. Under the gaudy festive canopies and bright lights, a *natchwali*[2] looks very glamorous. But for that first, holiest-of-holy exchange of glances in wedlock, the bride's face has to be framed with a Banarasi[3] veil: the special has to be seen in a special light. The garish canopy expresses fashion, the Banarasi veil conveys style. Amit declares that in our country, people are not over-fond of style. They are nervous about moving off the well-beaten, tested track leading to easy popularity. The Puranic[4] story narrating Daksha's[5] great sacrifice bears testimony to the truth of this statement. The fashionable gods, Indra, Chandra, Varuna, got invited everywhere – even at Daksha's sacrifice. Siva had style, his inimitable originality scared off the patrons. They instinctively

---

[2] Women, who danced in public to entertain the Bengali elite and the middle-classes. They represented an intrinsic angle of the babu-culture in nineteenth-century Bengal.

[3] Beautiful woven textiles, particularly silks, from Benares in United Provinces (modern-day Uttar Pradesh).

[4] There are eighteen Mahapuranas, compiled in the ancient period in India, and another eighteen minor Puranas but scholars have concluded that there are many more. At a conservative estimate, there might be eighty-two major and minor Puranas. These are not necessarily Hindu texts for there are Jain texts too. They have been composed not just in Sanskrit but also in the regional vernaculars.

[5] Daksha or skilful, was born from Brahma's right thumb. Another version from the *Rig Veda* states that Daksha was generated by Aditi and Aditi from Daksha. He was Sati's father. Sati became Siva's wife.

fathomed Siva's unconventionality and shunned him. I like listening to such pontifications from an Oxonian, for I certainly believe I've got style. The proof lies in the single-edition life-span of my books – they never reappear.

Nabakrishna, my brother-in-law, found Amit's opinions infuriating. He would often dismissively snort, 'Hang your Oxford graduates!' As the proud owner of a post-graduate degree in English Literature, he had been taught to grind away at learned tomes, not to understand them. Only the other day he complained to me, 'Amit delights in elevating the small-fries of literature merely to belittle the better-known ones. His hobby is to drum up support for his deliberate insolence, and you're his drummer-boy.' Unfortunately for him, his sister happens to be my wife. She heard it and vociferously objected to such prejudices, much to my intense satisfaction. I have further noted her wholehearted support for Amit's views, though she has not received much education. The natural intelligence of womankind is truly remarkable!

Occasionally though, I too have felt a niggling doubt about Amit's opinions, particularly when he waves away even great names in English literature – the kind whose presence simply looms over the market! One can get away with blindly singing their praises without ever opening a page! Amit also considers reading their literary efforts unnecessary for the holy act of criticism. He holds well-known authors to be too establishment-prone, rather like the waiting-room at the Bardhaman railway station. Characteristically, the authors he has discovered for himself he considers exclusively his, much like private salons in special trains.

Amit is addicted to style. This shows not just in his literary proclivities, but also in his sartorial tastes and general attitude. He is what you would call 'distinguished'. He is sure to catch your eye in a crowd. A clean-shaven, glossily dark face sparkling with merriment, bright eyes, bright laughter, restless movements and a gift for quick repartee: a flint-like mind which emits a veritable shower of sparks at a tap. He is into indigenous clothes because no one in his social circle wears them. He sports a white *dhoti,* carefully pleated in the old-fashioned manner, as his age-group considers such garb unthinkable. He wears quaint kurtas, with buttons running down obliquely from the left shoulder to the right side of his waist, and with sleeves slit picturesquely from wrist to elbow. A broad, brown-and-zari-worked band encircles his waist. His pocket-watch rests within a small, patterned pouch, slung from the band's left side. White leather sandals with inserts of red leather-strips encase his feet. A shawl dangles from his left shoulder to his knee when he sails forth from his house. When out visiting friends, a white Muslim fez from Lucknow completes this ensemble. I won't call this dandyism, but Amit's special brand of uproarious laughter. I don't profess to understand Western sartorial styles. But the knowledgeable assure me that Amit's carefully-achieved dishevelled appearance is considered to be in the right mode. His eccentricities are not adopted to enhance his personal charms, but to mock prevailing fashions. You may see many who are formally classified under 'youth' because of their age. Amit's youth springs from pure youthfulness, totally reckless, holding nothing back, uncalculating, sweeping all before it like a tidal wave.

He has two sisters — Sissy and Lissy, new products in a new market — gift-wrapped in the latest fashion from head to toe. Complete to a shade in high heels, stringed coral and amber beads peeking from tightly-fitting lace-edged jackets, saris obliquely and closely hugging their bodies. They move clickety-click, speak in high tones, laugh in musical octaves, shoot flirtatious glances and quick, shy smiles and certainly know the value of deep, meaningful glances. They also flutter their pink fans before their faces, perch on sofa-arms where their men-friends lounge, and to their playful daring they retaliate with equally playful scolds, accompanied by light taps of their fans.

Male hearts fill with envy at Amit's success as a ladies' man. He has no particular partiality for any one — indeed, his enthusiasm generously includes the entire sex. Amit is not short of feminine company, so he isn't frantic for it. He is a regular at parties, participates in card-games, deliberately loses bets, pleads soulfully with particularly tone-deaf ladies for more songs and is mustard-keen to know, from women wearing really garish colours, the names and location of the shops they patronise. His tone takes on a special inflection for each and every female acquaintance. Yet nobody is deceived — they all know his is an impartial partiality. A person sincerely devoted to many gods and goddesses, elevates each secretly to the top. The divinities are wise to the manouevre but are also pleased. Hopeful mothers continue hoping, but the daughters have figured out the elusive and tantalising quality of this constantly receding horizon. Amit ponders the feminine mystique, but is unable to come to a conclusion. He can nonchalantly strike up friendships with all and sundry and remains totally intrepid while treading the dangerous path to female friendship. Because of this, he never ever runs the risk of getting singed, despite his close range to such highly inflammable material.

Just the other day at a picnic, when the new moon rose over the still darkness piled high on the other bank of the Ganga, Lily Ganguly happened to be at his side. He told her softly, 'The new moon on that bank of the Ganga, you and I on this bank – such a unique concourse will never recur in an eternity'.

Lily's heart leapt for a moment. Still, she knew the only truth in this declaration lay in the artful utterance. To claim more would be to claim the iridescent shimmer on a bubble. She quickly regained her poise, and laughingly parried, 'Amitt, what you said was so true you needn't have said it. Just now that frog leaped into the water – this, too, will not recur in an eternity'.

Amit laughed too – 'Lily, there is a difference, a huge difference. This evening, that frog's leap is totally accidental. But you and I, the moon, the stars, the flow of the Ganga, all blend into symphonic perfection – Beethoven's Moonlight Sonata[6].

---

[6] Ludwig van Beethoven (1770–1827), composed 32 piano sonatas, and the Moonlight Sonata is one of the more famous piano solos.

There is a divine lunatic of a jeweller in Visvakarma's[7] workshop who casts moments in perfect golden circlets of time, studded with the rarest of gems, and then flings them away irretrievably into the sea – no one can ever find them again.'

'That's very convenient for you, Amitt, you won't have to pay Visvakarma's bills'.

'But Lily, if, after millions of years, you and I met on the banks of a thousand-kilometre long canal along the shady red glades of Mars, and that fisherman from *Shakuntala*[8] suddenly startled us with the ring, what then?'

Lily's fan became playfully active on Amit's arm – 'Then the golden ring would again vanish into the sea. Another creation by that divine lunatic will be added to the numbers you have already forgotten.'

So saying, Lily hurriedly left for the safer company of her friends. This is just one example of the many encounters Amit normally enjoyed with the opposite sex. His sisters, Sissy and Lissy, ask him – 'Ami, why don't you get married?' Amit is flippant, 'The most urgently-required ingredient in a marriage is the bride, the groom is secondary.'

---

[7] Visvakarma, the architect of the Devas, and the son of Prabhasa, the eighth of the eight Vasus and Varasri, the sister of Brhaspati.

[8] Kalidasa, flourished 5th century AD, Sanskrit poet and dramatist, probably the greatest Indian writer of any epoch. One of the major dramas he wrote was Abhijñāna Śakuntala ('The Recognition of Śakuntalā).

Sissy retorts, 'Surprising statement, considering there is a long queue of girls.'

'In the olden days,' Amit returns, 'girls were married off in strict accordance with what was auspicious. I want a bride whose personality will be her introduction, who will be unique, the only one of her kind in the whole wide world.'

Sissy tries again, 'As soon as she crosses your threshold, her identity will merge with yours, you will come first.'

'The girl for whom I vainly wait is not fixed to an address. Quite often, her feet do not turn homeward. She is like a falling star, and ignites as soon as she comes in contact with a throbbing heart, she does not touch the earthy space of domesticity,' Amit maintains perversely.

Sissy is ruffled – 'Meaning, she is not one little bit like your sisters'.

Amit rebuts instantly, 'Meaning, upon arrival, she does not merely add to the number of family members.'

Lissy tries another tack, 'Dear Sissy, Bimi Bose is simply yearning for Ami – at just a hint, she'll come running. But does Ami like her? Oh, no! He says she does not have culture, yet she stood first in MA Botany. Knowledge is culture.'

Amit protests, 'Knowledge is an invaluable diamond, but a stone as well. The light beaming from it is culture. The stone is heavy, the light alone dazzles.'

'Isssh! Bimi Bose has no worth in his eyes!' Lissy, annoyed, snaps – 'As if he's worthy of her! Even if Ami madly longs to wed her, I'll warn her not to give him a look!'

Amit provocatively replies, 'Only if I ran mad would I want to marry Bimi Bose. In that case, get me help, don't think of my nuptials!'

His relatives have finally given up thoughts of Amit's marriage, and have concluded he is too fickle for that blessed state. He just builds castles in the air, and likes shocking people with his deliberate perversity. His uncontrollable mind shimmers like a mirage, and can easily mislead one.

Meanwhile, the undeterred Amit rampages through town at will: takes this nonentity to Firpo for tea, takes that bunch of nobodies for a motor-car-ride, buys indiscriminately and gifts them away nonchalantly. He purchases English books and leaves them at other peoples' houses, supremely indifferent about their retrieval.

His sisters, however, are really incensed with his habit of holding contradictory positions in polite gatherings in the face of prevailing opinions. Once, some political scientist was pontificating on the merits of democracy, and of course Amit had a ready comment – 'When Vishnu carved Sati's body into pieces,[9] scattering them across the earth, more than a hundred

---

[9] Sati was indignant at the deliberate omission of Siva from Daksha's sacrifice, and gave up her body. Siva destroyed Daksha's sacrifice in his fury, and danced the tandava with Sati's body. Vishnu put an end to Siva's tandava by cutting it into pieces. There are various opinions on the number of pieces. Estimates vary between 5-100. The standard view is that there were 52 pieces, and 52 pithas. Still, it is unanimous that the vulva fell on Kamarupa and became one of the major pithas.

pilgrimages sprang up at these spots. Similarly, democracy has littered the entire country today with petty aristocracies and slavishly worships them. These aristocracies have mushroomed all over the world – some in politics, some in literature, some in society. But they are lightweight air-bubbles, for they do not believe in themselves.'

Another day, another incident. Some chivalrous champion of women was busy enumerating the imperfections of men. Amit, removing his cigarette from his lips, butted in: 'As soon as men step down from power, women will rule. The rule of the weak is highly dangerous.'

The ladies and their knights reacted instantaneously and sharply – 'Just what do you mean?'

Amit, undaunted, said, 'The group possessing chains can forcibly shackle a bird, visibly employing power. Those without, use drugs – the opium of illusion. The chain-wielders use coercion to confine but practice no deception. The seductresses, with opium as their weapon, not only confine but also enchant, while that witch, Nature, assiduously tends to the line of fresh supplies.'

To give another example. For the first time in his life, Amit had agreed to chair an evening session for the Literary Association in Ballygunge. The sole intellectual agenda was Robi Thakur's poetry. Amit had mentally armed himself for the occasion. An old-fashioned, good natured old fogy was the speaker. To his and the others' satisfaction, he proved that Robi Thakur's poetry *was* poetry. Only a few dubious professorial faces registered dour disagreement. The Chairman did more. He stood up and said, 'The careers of all poets should be limited to five years. We ask for variety, not more of the same. When seasons run dry of the delicious Fajli mangoes, we don't insist on a better breed of Fajli. Instead we demand, "Hey, get really good custard apples from the market!" Unlike the meaty ripe coconuts, green coconuts don't last long. Nevertheless, we aesthetically appreciate the flavour of green coconuts too. Likewise, poets have a brief run, unlike hoary-headed philosophers, who chug along, regardless of age. My greatest complaint against Robi Thakur is that he follows that old Wordsworth[10] in leading a tiresomely long life. Yama has sent him notice to quit long ago. But the fellow, even while reluctantly half-rising from his chair, stubbornly clings to its handles. If he doesn't realise he has overstayed his welcome, we should leave the assembly as our bounden duty. The next arrival on the scene will be equally determined to reign eternally. He also will nourish expectations that a this-worldly Amaravati[11] will be fastened forever to only *his* gatepost. The devotees should prepare to worship for a short while at this new alter with garlands and grub. They should then make suitable arrangements to sacrifice this new god to mark the

---

[10]William Wordsworth (1770–1850), the English poet was part of the Romantic movement in literature.

[11]Amaravati is the capital of swarga, the heavenly abode of the gods, situated on Mount Meru. Here Indra reigned as the king of the devas

auspicious moment of their freedom from their devotional bonds. In Africa, four-legged gods are sacrificed on the same principles. Two-legged, three-legged, four-legged, even the fourteen-legged gods, ritually share the same fate. When an act of worship turns into a boring routine, it is the greatest blasphemy of all. Liking is evolutionary. If, something likeable remains unchanged for five years, it is high time its obituary was written. Quite possibly, the poor thing has not quite comprehended its own demise. The relatives, abstaining from giving an admonitory push, and postponing funereal rites, most probably have ulterior designs on the rightful successor's inheritance. I want to expose this fraud hatched by Robi Thakur's coterie for hoodwinking the public.'

Our Manibhushan, with a flash of his spectacles, demanded, 'You want loyalty to disappear from literature?'

'Certainly!' Amit affirmed intrepidly. 'From now on, the poet-as-President gets only a brief stint. My second contention against Robi Thakur's writing is that of effeminacy. His writing follows the rounded, wave-like formation of his script, resembling nothing so much as a rose, a female face, the moon. Its cast is taken from Nature's imprint, and is primitive. From the new President we demand bold, clear lines – like an arrow, a spear-head, a thorn, or a lightning-bolt – not flower-like, but sharp as pain! Like the pointed arches of a Gothic cathedral, not like the rounded temple shikharas! We wouldn't even object to strong resemblances to jute or flour mills, or even the Secretariat building! Abandon soft seduction, and abduct the mind, the way Ravana abducted Sita.[12] Even if the mind weeps and protests all the way, go it must. That old Jatayu[13], in an abortive rescue-bid, will have to die! Then, Kiskindhya[14] will awaken, Hanuman will leap on Lanka, and restore the mind to its former place. Then it will be the time for tearful reunions with Tennyson and Byron![15] We'll beg Dickens[16] to forgive us for abusing him. But it is necessary to break free from our self-induced literary trance. If, after the fashion of the Mughal emperors, hypnotised artists continue to create bubbles of marble, we, the bhadralok, will be driven to

---

[12] Sita was the daughter of King Janaka of Videha and the wife of Rama. She was abducted by Ravana, the king of the rakshasas, and taken to Lanka. The epic *Ramayana* narrates the story of Rama and Sita.

[13] According to the *Ramayana*, Jatayu was the son of Vishnu's vehicle, Garuda, and the king of the vultures. Alternatively, he was the son of Aruna. He fought Ravana when he was abducting Sita, but was mortally wounded in the combat. Still, he managed to tell Rama and Lakshmana what had befallen Sita, before he died.

[14] The capital city of the monkeys, with Bali, and later Sugriva, as its king.

[15] Alfred Tennyson (1809–1892), the poet laureate of Victorian England, very popular and his works were widely read, both in England and America.

George Gordon Byron, the 6th Lord (1788–1824) and an English poet belonging to the Romantic period. His *Childe Harold* set him on the road to fame.

[16] Charles Dickens (1812–1870), an acclaimed novelist of Victorian England. He wrote thirty-four major works and many more minor essays and stories.

banaprastha[17] before we cross twenty! Merely to appreciate the Taj Mahal, the sentimentalism surrounding it must go.'

(One must say here, that the reporter struggling to keep pace with this flood of words, often floundered out of his depth. What he finally got on paper was even more garbled than Amit's speech, if that was possible. Whatever fragments I could retrieve, I have arranged here, to the best of my ability.)

At this second reference to the Taj Mahal, a devotee of Robi Thakur, red with anger, blustered: 'The proliferation of good things is healthy.'

'Just the opposite!' Amit contradicted – 'In the creator's logic, excellence is dictated by rarity. Too much of good things would compel even the best to jostle for elbow room with a huge host of the mediocre. Those poets who shamelessly live on till seventy and beyond, punish themselves by cheapening themselves. At the end, a group of imitators around such figures turn all literary activity into a farce. The poet's writing deteriorates. He keeps borrowing from his previous works, and veritably turns into "a receiver of stolen property"! In such cases, for public good, it is our stern duty to kill off such poets. I am not talking of actual death but of their poetic demise. May the

---

[17] Vanaprastha is the third asrama or stage of the life of a householder. Under the law of Manu, the life of a Brahman was divided into four asramas – Brahmachar, Grihastha, Vanaprastha and Sannyasya. In Vanaprastha, the householder becomes a dweller in the forests, leading a life of self-denial and performing strictly all ceremonial duties.

old critics, the old politicians and the old teachers live twice as long.'

A more up-to-date spokesman challenged – 'So, who do you think would fit the bill for the President?'

'Nibaran Chakraborty,' Amit flashed.

A chorus of surprised voices arose from many chairs— 'Nibaran Chakraborty?! Who's he?'

'The answer to that question is a mere seedling today,' declared Amit, 'but tomorrow it will grow into a huge tree.'

'For now,' the audience demanded, 'we want a sample.'

'Then listen.' So saying, Amit produced a long, slim canvas-bound notebook and began to read:

'I announce an arrival unfamiliar on earth
before this motley assemblage, destined to remain a stranger
and a riddle.
Open the door, hear the divine words roll.

Mahakaleshwar[18] hurls the bolt of cryptic code,
demanding of the daring reckless
to hazard a reply, or to pay as forfeit, Death.

They won't obey. The armies of stupidity bar the way.
Their impotent rage, lashing angrily against themselves

---

[18] Mahakala or Mahakaleshwar is a synonym of Siva, the God of destruction. It also means the Lord of Time.

*like helpless waves incessantly dashing their heads
on stony banks, in the false pride of suicide.*

*Ungarlanded, bare-chested, unheralded,
Unadorned with mail, armlet, ear-pendant
On my forehead clearly blazoned
The message of victory.*

*Dressed in beggarly rags, I'll beggar your treasure.
Open the door. Suddenly my outthrust hand makes instant
demands.
Your soul shudders before your shivering door.
Your world rocks. The fearful scream in terror,
rending the horizon, 'Reckless indomitable beggar,
leave this moment. Your echoing voice,
booming through this still night, pierces it.*

*Bring your weapons. Smite at my breast.
Let Death kill Death. This deathless life
To you I'll gift.*

*Chain me. Tie me. In an instant such bonds will snap.
Your freedom is ordained
only at the moment of my liberation.*

*Challenge me with canonical texts?
Scholar to scholar, divine ordinations will tumble.*

I know arguments will crumble
Eyes will wrench free of ancient rote and behold the day.

Light a fire. If today's good loses strength tomorrow,
and turns to cinder, ashes and sorrow
Let it. Banish sadness.
In this ordeal by fire, the world will be recast afresh.

My harsh message falls with hammer-force on perverse
intellects,
Makes them start, terror-struck.
My mad rhythm creates chaos
For the minions of peaceful sloth, or the tired, ravenous
niggards.

My fist cuffing heads, will convince everybody
gripped in anger, regret and fear
within society – of the new herald's invincibility.
Unfathomable, unknowable is his identity.
A summer thunder-storm trampling the earth,
With iron-fist battling, wrestling from the clouds
their withheld plenty,
Tearing and liberating the whole world.'

Robi Thakur's coterie was silenced that evening and left with just enough wind to promise a written retaliation. When Amit was driving back home after stunning the audience, Sissy charged him – 'You must have concocted this Nibaran Chakraborty in advance to fool these well-meaning people.'

'The person who introduces a possibility, as yet a non-arrival, is his Creator. I'm that. Now that Nibaran Chakraborty has come down to earth, he will be unstoppable,' Amit announced triumphantly.

Sissy was inwardly very proud of Amit. 'Amit, do you think out all the sharp things you say the first thing in the morning, before you leave your bed?' she asked confidentially.

Amit said smugly, 'Civilisation is another name for being prepared for any possibility. The primitive is *always* unprepared across the globe. This is also recorded in my notebook'.

'But you don't *have* any opinion,' Sissy protested. 'You say whatever sounds good at the moment.'

'My mind has a mirror-like surface. It wouldn't catch and reflect every passing moment if I made the mistake of holding opinions,' returned Amit.

Sissy said protestingly, 'Ami, you will spend your life with reflections.'

Chapter 2
The Collision

*A*mit carefully selected the Shillong hills for his holiday. Reason – no one from his social circle ever ventured there. Another compelling reason – the tidal wave of hopeful mothers and marriageable daughters turned into a manageable trickle there. The naughty god, who kept up a steady barrage of well-directed arrows at his unsusceptible heart, preferred more fashionable urban quarters. All the resorts tucked away in unfashionable hilly bosoms presented him with constricted opportunities for target practice. His sisters had flatly refused such uninspiring surroundings and had sniffed, 'Go if you want. We certainly shan't.'

The sisters sped off to Darjeeling, fashionable parasols dangling from a hand, tennis racquets held in another, with artificial Persian cloaks providing the finishing touch. Bimi Bose, already expectantly ensconced in Darjeeling, suddenly discovered that though Darjeeling was choked with people, there was no company. The sisters had arrived without the brother. Meanwhile, Amit had announced to all his lofty intention of enjoying unadulterated solitude. Before two days had crept leadenly by, he realised the emptiness of such sheer solitude, unleavened by an appreciative audience. Neither could he bring himself to roam around with camera in hand: how often he himself had scoffed, 'I'm not a tourist! I have no desire to gobble things with my eyes, I want to taste them with my mind!'

For a few days he managed to read under the shady Deodar trees. Characteristically, he stubbornly stuck to Suniti Chattopadhyay's[19] exposition of Bengali phonetics, hoping he would be granted an opportunity to differ with the author. Occasionally, the grand beauty of his surroundings held him spellbound, even though his restless mind alternated fitfully between bouts of lethargy and reading. Unfortunately, in this opulent display of natural beauty, there was no focal point. For Amit, it remained a monotonous background note. There was too much variety. Without an underlying grand theme, the plenitude dissolved in a mere agglomerate of the many. Amit's own mind reflected this unfocused, distracting abundance, as it constantly searched for some universal principle which would

---

[19]Suniti Chattopadhyay (1890–1976), a professor of languages and also a well-known Indologist in Calcutta University.

aid the convergence of his thoughts. Here, amidst all this reverberating grand silence, his quicksilver mind could not dissipate itself in the constant urban round of social activities. It rapidly became entrapped within itself and suffocatingly heightened his innate restlessness, like a dammed waterfall inevitably turning into a lake. That's when he began to seriously consider bolting from the hills. He contemplated a valiant flight in a wide detour, all the way through Silchar and Sylhet, and finally beating a game retreat into his own world. And the monsoon descended as if on cue, trailing its dark veil, hovering in dark magnificence over mountains and forests, and threatening to drown Cherrapunji in torrential rain. It certainly drowned Amit's restlessness, firing him with the desire to compose another *Meghadutam*[20], with a nameless heroine so dazzling, so bewitching, elusive and capricious, she would captivate all.

Chasing his thoughts, that day he pulled on knee-length pants, a khaki Norfolk shirt, Highland socks, thick-soled boots, and crowned his efforts with a solar topee. In this attire, he resembled more a district engineer out on supervision than Abani Thakur's[21] picturesque representation of the bereaved yaksha[22] in *Meghadutam*. Still, his pockets bulged with some five

---

[20] *Megahdutam* (The Cloud Messenger) is a major work by Kalidasa.

[21] Abani or Abanindranath Thakur (1871–1951), Rabindranath's cousin. He started a new school of painting in nineteenth-century Bengal. He also wrote for children.

[22] Yaksha belonged to a class of supernatural beings attendant on Kuvera, the god of wealth. Kalidasa uses the grief of a yaksha separated from his wife in his poem, *Mcghadutam*.

or six slim volumes of poetry in various languages, at odds with his appearance.

He drove fast and recklessly on the mountain roads, for there was no danger of oncoming traffic. On the right side of the twisting road, the cliffs dropped sharply down. His thoughts veered fancifully towards the car as the modern messenger of love to the adored woman of his epic. It had just the right combination of light, smoke, water and wind, while a letter to the driver would leave nothing to chance misinterpretations. As swift as his lively imagination, he instantly determined that the monsoon the following year would see him driving down the very roads described in that epic poetry. Who knew, the Fates might cast in his way an Avantika or a Malavika or a forest-nymph, preserved solely for him out of the aeons of time! Suddenly, on rounding a sharp bend, he saw a car coming up the road. There was no room to manoeuvre. Stepping on the brakes did not prevent his car from moving forward. A collision was unavoidable. That there were no ensuing fatalities, was providential. The other car rolled back a little under the impact, but the mountain shoulder firmly halted it.

A girl stepped out of the car and stood framed against the stark possibility of imminent death. Etched clearly against this grim background, she was as distinct from her environment as a flash of lightning. Rising above the swelling waves of the fresh-churned seas still heaving from Mandar Parvat's[23] mighty efforts,

---

[23]Mandar Parvat was a great mountain which the Devas and the Asuras used for the churning of the ocean.

Lakshmi[24] appeared in all her splendour. Amit saw her in a rare moment. In a drawing room, among five other girls, she would not have been revealed in all her uniqueness. In this world, one can see many worthy people, but not in a place worthy of them.

She wore a thin-bordered sari of a white, woollen material, a matching jacket, white leather sandals in an indigenous design. She was tall and slim, with a golden-brown complexion, large, deep eyes shaded by long lashes, hair drawn back from a beautiful broad brow in a chignon. Her face, with its rounded chin, was as beautiful as a half-ripe fruit. The sleeves covered her arms to the elbow, two plain bangles adorned her forearms. Her sari, unpinned, covered her head, and was secured to her chignon with a silver hairpin of Kataki craftsmanship.

Amit left his topee in his car and stood quietly in front of her. He was plainly expecting a reprimand. Observing this, the girl felt a twinge of compassion, touched perhaps with a dash of amusement. In low tones, Amit apologised, 'It was completely my fault.'

The girl smiled and replied, 'Not a fault, but a mistake. And I made the mistake first.' The girl's voice had the musical exuberance and fullness of rippling water gushing from its source. It had the tonal clarity of a young boy's voice. After coming back to his rooms that evening, Amit went into a

---

[24] Lakshmi or Sri (in later times) is the Goddess of fortune, wife of Vishnu, and mother of Kama. According to the *Ramayana* she emerged from the sea of milk as it was being churned by the Devas and the Asuras.

prolonged mental search for a suitable analogy to describe the tangible quality of the voice with that special flavour. He finally wrote in his notebook, 'It was like the specially textured smoke of Amboori[25] tobacco, swirling through the water of a hookah. It did not have the acrid tang of nicotine, but carried instead the gentle scent of rose-water'.

The girl explained why she was caught on the wrong side – 'I was looking for a friend who has turned up here. The chauffeur had warned me a little way up this path that this could not be the road. But by then there was no way of turning back, and we had to go on. We were climbing up until your appearance forced us to stop.'

Amit said, 'There are top-dogs set above ordinary top dogs – which in this case is a wicked planetary configuration. That is responsible for this misdeed.'

The chauffeur announced his presence at this point with his assessment of the situation, 'There is very little damage, but it will take a while to set it right.'

Amit quickly offered, 'If you can forgive my erring car, I can drop you wherever you were planning to go.'

'It won't be necessary. I'm used to walking on mountain paths,' said she.

'The necessity is mine. I want proof of your forgiveness,' persisted Amit.

---

[25] Amboori tobacco was from Ambur, a city famous for tobacco and essence of flowers or attar.

The doubtful girl remained quiet. Amit pleaded, 'Let me add to my request. I drive – not a particularly grand occupation – for it certainly does not lead straight to the doors of posterity. But so far this is my only introduction in your eyes. But even that has backfired. Let me demonstrate in the epilogue that I am at least as worthy as your chauffeur.'

Normally girls, fearful of unknown dangers, are wary of strangers at their first meeting. But the dangerous collision had knocked some of the preliminary fences out of the way. Some fate, in these quiet hill roads, had compelled these two to halt. With invisible knots, it had hastily fastened the memory of this meeting within their minds. The suddenness of it resembled highlighted forms under a lightning-flash. From now on, when jerked out of sleep, their minds would frequently dwell on these impressions. Like a cosmic impact which generated the tremendous energy that converged into myriad blazing stars in the firmament, it burnt deep imprints upon their consciousness.

Without further words, the girl got into Amit's car. Following her instructions, the car reached its destination without mishap. She then descended from it, and politely invited Amit, 'If you have time tomorrow, please do come over and meet my Kartama.'[26]

Amit almost hopped out with an eager, 'I don't lack time, I can come this instant,' but for once remained tongue-tied with embarrassment. Back home, Amit conversed with his notebook:

---

[26] Kartama or the Bengali equivalent of the mistress of an establishment.

'What sudden lunacy on the part of the Road. It tore out two different persons from two totally different situations, and threw them together on the same path. The astronomer was certainly wrong. The moon must have accidentally fallen into the earth's gravitational field — like a cosmic car accident which had threatened to obliterate both — and since then both have always moved together, mutually shedding light on each other. Tied together in movement. My mind tells me, maybe our paired movement has begun. On that ever-moving thread we will string bright, just-found moments. The chance to get stuck with a fixed salary and a fixed ration will vanish. All our give-and-take will be negotiated suddenly.'

It was raining outside. Pacing rapidly up and down the verandah Amit muttered to himself, 'Where are you, Nibaran Chakraborty? Possess me now, give me words. Words!' Out came the long, slim notebook, and Nibaran Chakraborty declaimed,

> *'The way was paved with knotless strings*
> *We are two riders upon the winds,*
> *Colourful moments beloved of dust,*
> *with red powder colour our hearts,*
> *The monsoon clouds, with flying veils,*
> *Dance like the diganganas[27];*
> *Sudden-light flashing by*
> *Makes our minds sparkle.*

---

[27]Diganganas are celestial female forms present at the eight points of the compass.

> *Not for us any kanak-champa glen*
> *Or wild-flowers' strewn bakul[28]-glade.*
> *At dusk, suddenly some*
> *Nameless flower's perfumed breath*
> *Or the red lances of rhododendrons*
> *Atop the green branches long,*
> *Beside which the rosy morning clouds*
> *Can easily look jaded and pale.*
>
> *Hoarded treasures we possess not,*
> *Of domestic care and nurture we know naught.*
> *On the road the bird on the wing*
> *We leave uncaged to freely sing,*
> *Our happiness wells at their outspread-wings,*
> *at the calls of these freedom-loving sprites.*
> *The unimaginable's sudden aura sets us alight.'*

Now here we have to backtrack a little. For the story to actually move forward, a quick backward glance at the past is necessary.

---

[28] Kanak-champa is a light yellow coloured flower, with a beautiful perfume. Bakul is a small white flower with a heavy scent.

Chapter 3
Preface

When Bengal was going through the first stages of English education, the old air from the Chandimandaps[29] mingled with the hot, strong winds emanating from the schools and colleges, and created pressure pockets. By and by, these turned actively into whirlwinds of social rebellion, and Jnanadashankar was one person who succumbed willingly to its force. Though he formally belonged to a traditional time-zone, his dates slid forward quite a bit. He was far ahead of his times. In intellect, speech and action, he

---

[29]Chandimandap was a structure paved with stones, under the peepul tree of the village temple dedicated to the Goddess Chandi, another form of Durga. This is where the village elders normally gathered.

was totally unlike his contemporaries. Like sea-birds revelling in the constantly rolling waves, he revelled in the wash of constant social criticism which inevitably came his way.

Generally, the grandsons of such grandfathers, desirous of resetting chronology back into the right temporal context, take a huge running leap straight back inside the almanac's most orthodox terminus. This is precisely what happened here as well. Jnanadashankar's grandson Barodashankar, if measured according to the prevalent norms in society, could certainly be said to resemble the primitive ancestors of his father and grandfather. He turned with folded hands to Manasa[30], and, called Shitala[31] mother, in order to take the edge off her temper. The practice of drinking water consecrated with holy amulets began anew. Mornings rolled away just writing Durga's[32] name a thousand times. The Vaishya communities, trying to claim Brahminical status in his area, were shoved back into their proper mental and social orbits. He unstintingly flooded modern-day intellects with freely distributed religious pamphlets filled with the pronouncements of the Rishis of yore to rescue Hindutva

---

[30] Manasa was the sister of the serpent Sesha and wife of the sage Jarat karu. She is also called Jagadgauri, Nitya (eternal) and Padmavati. She had special powers in counteracting the venom of serpents, and was also called Visha-hari.

[31] Shitala was the Goddess of diseases like small-pox and cholera.

[32] Durga was the wife of Siva, daughter of Himavat. As the Sakti or female energy of Siva she has two characters, one mild and the other fierce, and it is as the latter or Durga that she is especially worshipped.

from the polluting rationality of modern western science. The Bhatpara press provided the ammunition. In a short while, he managed to erect an impenetrable fortress, encased in ritual purity. It was formidably barricaded behind rites and rituals, meditations and prayers, yoga and ritual cleansing, bathing, incense-burning, and the reverencing of cows and Brahmins. Finally, bearing the innumerable blessings of countless Brahmins, in exchange for all his gifts of cows, land, gold, defrayal of the costs of daughters' marriages, and of funeral rites for deceased fathers and mothers, he left for the other world. Then he was just twenty-seven years old.

Barodashankar's father and his boon companion, Ramlochan Barujje[33], had been fast friends all through college. They had even tasted the forbidden culinary delights like chops and cutlets in hotels together. Barujje's daughter, Yogamaya, became Barodashankar's wife. At this point, there were no behavioural dissimilarities between Yogmaya's paternal and in-laws' families. In Yogamaya's paternal home, girls not just studied and moved out-of-doors, but some had even authored illustrated travel accounts in established journals. Her husband was constantly on the watch to ensure that a girl from such a background did not short-change the deities by omitting even a single rite. Any transgression of the Sanatana[34] tradition, which might threaten

---

[33] Barujje is the colloquial form of Bandopadhyay. The anglicised versions are Bannerjee/Banerji/Bonerji.

[34] Sanatana is commonly understood as the authentic Brahminical tradition.

its fragile boundaries, was unthinkable. Yogmaya's movements were strictly curtailed by its iron rules. The veil descended not just over her eyes, but over her mind as well. If the Goddess Saraswati ever managed to come inside the house during her leisure hours, even she had to shake out her clothes at the check-post. Any book which was contemporary to, or belonged to the post-Bankim phase of Bengali literature, could not cross the threshold with her. As for any English books, they had to be abandoned outside the house. The critical edition of *Yogavashistha Ramayana*[35] had been sitting on Yogmaya's shelf for a long time. The young household patriarch had died with the unalloyed anxiety that she might hold an erudite discussion on that to while away her time. In this puranic iron safe, Yogamaya had kept her rebellious mind under firm control like a tucked-away safe-deposit, but it had not been easy for her. Her only solace in this rigorous imprisonment of the mind had been the family pandit in residence – Dinasharan Vedantaratna. Yogamaya's crystal-clear, natural intelligence had greatly appealed to him. He used to say quite openly, 'Ma[36], all this rubbish of fasts and observances are not for you. The stupid not only manage to cheat themselves, but they are fooled by everything in this world. Do you think we ourselves really

---

[35] *Yogavashista Ramayana* of Valmiki, is a part of the Vedanta, where the kulguru of the Iksvakus, Vasista, expounded on the *Ramayana* to Rama.
[36] 'Ma' or 'mother' is a special endearment used by Bengalis. Elderly people generally use it to address young women

believe in all this? Why do you think that when it comes to pronouncing some decisions, we use grammatical subtleties to twist meanings to suit ourselves, and don't even feel remotely sorry? This in itself implies that in our heart of hearts, we are not bound by these rules. Only to fool people, we have to appear foolish. But since you refuse to be blinkered, I can't and won't hoodwink you. Ma, whenever you feel inclined to question anything, send for me. Whatever I think I know as the truth from the *Shastras*, I will frankly discuss with you.'

And so it was that occasionally Vedantaratna would exegetically draw from the *Gita*, or the *Brahmobhashya* and Yogamaya's insightful questions would send him into ecstasies. His enthusiasm for further intellectual discussions with Yogamaya knew no bounds. He had nothing but contempt for the large community of gurus, that Barodashankar had gathered around him. He used to tell Yogamaya, 'Ma, only here, in the whole of this big city, do I find intellectual satisfaction in discussion. You have saved me from self-castigation.' Existence, crowded with unremitting rituals and fasts, leaden with the chains fashioned by the almanac, somehow dragged on. Life, in the horrendous vocabulary of the modern-day press, was measured out in 'rule-bound obedience'. Immediately after her husband's death, Yogamaya stepped out of the home with her son Jyotishankar, and daughter, Surama. Winters she spent in Calcutta, and during the summers, she normally chose some hill-resort. Jyotishankar was now in college. For Surama's education, after an immense search for someone suitable, as she disapproved of the kind of girls' schools on offer, Yogamaya had managed to get Labanyalata. Amit had met Labanyalata accidentally this morning.

Chapter 4

Labanya's History

Labanya's father, Abanish Dutta, was a professor in some college in western India. He had brought up his motherless girl in a manner that had withstood all the friction of passing examinations. Even more remarkably, neither her intelligence nor her quest for knowledge had been destroyed. Her desire to read remained undiminished.

The father's great love was scholarship. All his passion for it was expressed in his encouragement of his daughter's literary leanings. And he loved her even more than his library. He firmly believed that if someone pursued knowledge with true devotion, all the cracks from which vaporous longings might arise, would be hermetically sealed. Marriage could never be necessary for that person. He was absolutely convinced that his daughter's mind had turned to solidified concrete with mathematics and history. There was no soft, fertile, even mildly suitable, corner left in it for the harvest of love and service to a husband. One could certainly call it a firm strong mind – if it was scratched from the outside, it would not leave a mark. He had even let his mind hover on the thought that it didn't matter if Labanya never married – she could be tied in holy matrimony to scholarship instead.

Only one other person received Abanish Dutta's wholehearted affection. His name was Shobhanlal. Indeed it was rare to see someone so young so totally engrossed in study. In his wide forehead, his frank eyes, his sweet and innocent smile, his youthful face, there was something which drew immediate attention. Inordinately bashful, Shobhanlal often disintegrated with confusion at the merest hint of any attention.

The son of a poor man, he leaped from examination to examination effortlessly, balancing himself on the steps of a series of student scholarships. His professor had deep pride in him. He secretly hoped that when Shobhan really struck it big in the academic world, his own name would top the list of people who had helped him to fame. Shobhan frequented his house for lessons and had free access to his library. On these visits, whenever he came across Labanya, he would almost cower in embarrassment. Because his self-deprecating embarrassment was distancing, Labanya's conviction that she was better than Shobhanlal on the intellectual scale remained unshaken. When a man, suffering from feelings of self-doubt, does not assert his own worth, women also fail to perceive him with any degree of clarity.

It was then that Nanigopal, Shobhanlal's father, descended on Abanish and soundly abused him. His chief complaint was that Abanish, using the poor excuse of professorial aid, had actually laid a matrimonial trap for a Vaidya's son. Such malignant designs would also fall in neatly with some easy-to-achieve social reform. As incontrovertible proof, he produced a pencil-sketch of Labanya, discovered damningly from the recesses of Shobhanlal's trunk, and covered thickly with rose petals. Nanigopal was completely convinced that the sketch was a loving gift from Labanya. Shobhanlal's father knew to a hair the present market-price of his son. More future academic laurels around the head of this fantastic matrimonial catch would surely enhance his economic value in the marriage market astronomically. That Abanish had targeted such a valuable piece of merchandise, with no intention of paying for it, added insult to injury. This was outright robbery, and was certainly no better than stealing money.

Till now, Labanya had been totally unaware of this secret altar, where someone daily paid homage to her image. From an untidy heap of magazines and pamphlets dumped in a corner of Abanish's library, Shobhanlal had rescued an old, forgotten photograph of Labanya. He had got an artist friend of his to sketch her portrait, and then quietly put it back. Even the roses, like his spontaneous, youthful love, had bloomed in a friend's garden, and certainly did not embody a sordid history of aggressive appropriation. Yet punishment struck this hapless lad down. With bent head, a red face, a hand secretly wiping away tears, he left the house in mental disarray. From afar he offered one last proof of his devotion, completely unnoticed by anyone but his maker. In the BA examination, Shobhanlal had stood first. Labanya had been placed third. This had caused her ego-wrenching agony for two reasons. First came Abanish's openly expressed respect for Shobhanlal's intellect, which certainly bit deep into Labanya. But what had added to her secret pain and humiliation was the knowledge that Abanish indeed held Shobhanlal very dear. She had tried her very best to outstrip Shobhanlal in open competition. When she couldn't, her resentment blazed up within her and forgiving that unwitting culprit became impossible. She was always nagged by a doubt that Shobhanlal had received much more help from her father, and hence the difference in examination results. And yet that young man had never approached Abanish on the subject of examinations. For quite some time after that, whenever Labanya's eyes fell on Shobhanlal, she would turn away and walk off. Now the MA examinations were fast approaching, and for Labanya there was still no hope of competing against Shobhan successfully. And yet she was successful. Even Abanish was surprised. Had Shobhanlal been a poet he would have filled volumes with verses. Instead, from his share of examination-marks, he had offered up a large slice for Labanya.

Then the student days ended. Around this time, Abanish realised with deep pain that hearts were unreliable organs –

including his own. Even if the brain, continually crammed with intellectual treats, remained well-behaved, emotions did not obey rules, they just crowded in. Abanish was then forty-seven. At this vulnerable age, a widow stormed straight into his heart, totally ignoring the ramparts of his library or the fortifications of his scholarship. The only thing standing in the way of marriage was Abanish's deep affection for his daughter. A great intellectual battle ensued with his desires. The poor man would determine to get down to hard intellectual activity, but some enchanting thought would take forcible possession of his mind and halt his study. He would be asked to write a critical essay on a truly tempting book on the Buddhist archaeological remains by the Modern Review – he would remain sitting in front of the unopened book, the very embodiment of a ruined Buddhist stupa[37], heavy with the silence of hundreds of years. The editor would get anxious. But such effects on the scholarly were inevitable. The very foundations of his mountainous pile of knowledge were shaking, assaulted by an unknown enemy. When an elephant steps unwittingly into quicksand, can there be any hope for its survival?

---

[37]Stūpas are Buddhist commemorative monuments which usually house sacred relics associated with the Buddha or other saintly persons; they are architectural symbols of the Buddha's parinirvāna, or death. The hemispherical form of the stūpa appears to have derived from pre-Buddhist burial mounds in India. Sanchi the Great Stūpa (2nd–1st century BC), is a famous example of this kind of architecture.

Only now, half-a-lifetime later, Abanish's heart knew misgivings and repentance. He felt that he had been so caught up with his books, he had been blind to his daughter's love for Shobhanlal. He was equally convinced that it would have been unnatural on his daughter's part not to love Shobhanlal. Now, for the general species called 'fathers' he felt a deep anger – with himself, with Nanigopal!

Most opportunely, Abanish got a letter from Shobhan just then. Shobhan wanted to write an essay on the history of the Guptas[38] for the Premchand-Raichand Scholarship examination. He wished to borrow a few books from his professor's library. Thrilled, Abanish immediately wrote back an effusive assent, 'Of course you must work in my library like you used to, without feeling any hesitation.'

Shobhanlal's hopes suddenly soared. Only Labanya's tacit consent could be behind such an enthusiastic letter from his professor. He began to frequent the library again. In his numerous comings and goings, he would occasionally run into Labanya. Shobhan would expectantly slow down his pace a little. He fervently wished she would talk to him about something;

---

[38] The Guptas were the rulers of the Magadha state in northeastern India, later Bihār. They maintained an empire over northern and parts of central and western India from the early 4th to the late 6th century AD. The founder was Chandra Gupta I (q.v.). The Gupta era produced the decimal system of notation and great Sanskrit epics and Hindu art and contributed to the sciences of astronomy, mathematics, and metallurgy.

maybe just ask him, how he was. Possibly just express some curiosity about the essay he was working on. If she did, he would immediately open his notebook and launch forth into a discussion that would release all his pent-up feelings. He was filled with hopeful excitement at Labanya's probable observations on some of his conclusions based on hard research. But so far, there had been no such exchange of views, and he did not have the courage to advance on his own any conversational gambit.

A few days went by. Sunday came. Shobhanlal had his notebooks spread out before him, and was turning over the leaves of a book, occasionally taking notes. It was afternoon, the room was deserted. As it was a holiday, Abanish had gone off to some house he was careful not to name. He had just left word that he would not be back for tea. Suddenly the door opened noisily. Shobhanlal's heart gave a huge leap and then began to shiver in excitement. Labanya came in. Shobhan, highly agitated, leapt up in wordless bemusement. Labanya, exuding red-hot rage, demanded, 'Just why do you come to this house?'

Shobhanlal started, and could not think of any reply.

'Do you know what your father accused us of because you would keep coming here? Do you have no regard for how I may be humiliated?'

Shobhan lowered his eyes and almost whispered, 'Please forgive me, I will leave at once.'

He did not tell her that he had actually been invited by her father. He gathered his notebooks together with a shaking hand.

The dumb pain, forcing itself through his ribs, had no exit. He left the house with his head bent.

If some insuperable obstacle rises in the way of loving someone a great deal, and the right opportunity just gets wasted, the end-result is not a lukewarm feeling like not-loving. It is transformed into powerful, blind resentment, the other side of love. Perhaps, unknown even to her, Labanya was waiting graciously to bestow her hand on Shobhanlal herself. Shobhanlal did not respond in a very overt way. The subsequent flow of events went totally against him. This tragic finale hit him the hardest and the cruellest blow. Labanya, in her anguish, quite unfairly misjudged her father. She concluded that her father, wanting to be released from his responsibilities towards her, had deliberately recalled Shobhanlal so that the star-crossed, youthful pair could be united in wedlock. All her dammed-up fury therefore burst out in full blast against that guiltless lad.

Upon her insistence, Abanish found himself marrying the lady of his choice in the days that followed. It was only then that Labanya declared her intention of rejecting her father's carefully saved money, half of which he had set aside for her exclusive use, and making her own independent way in the world. Deeply hurt, Abanish said, 'I got married at your insistence, Labanya. On my own I wouldn't have taken such a step. Then why are you abandoning me in such a fashion?'

Labanya did not waver, but replied, 'I have resolved on this course only because I don't want to loosen the bond between us. Don't worry, father! Instead, give me your constant blessings so that I can follow the path which will give me true happiness.'

Labanya got a job. Surama's entire education was in her hands. She could have easily taught Jyoti, but that young man flatly refused to be subjected to the indignity of a female tutor.

In the daily routine of work, life flowed past in a fairly even-paced manner. Her leisure hours were totally taken up with English literature, from the ancient times to the current trends represented by Bernard Shaw[39], and especially with the Greek and Roman histories written by Grote[40], Gibbon[41], Gilbert[42]

---

[39] Bernard Shaw (1856–1950), the famous English dramatist, critic and intellectual, who influenced both the English and the colonial thinkers on the major social and intellectual problems of the day.

[40] George Grote (1794–1871), the son of George Grote (senior), a man who came to London from Bremen in the mid-eighteenth century, and became a rich merchant in London. George Grote junior was held to be an authority on the history of Greece. His work *History of Greece* was accepted as scholarly by most of English intellectuals of the day – James Mill, and his son, J.S. Mill. He had begun his work in 1822 and had finally published it in 1846.

[41] Edward Gibbon (1737–1794) was the son of Edward Gibbon (senior) a Tory Parliamentarian. Gibbon became very interested in the history of Rome when at Oxford. He is most famous for the *Decline and Fall of the Roman Empire*. He also wrote a four-volume *History of England*, which is still accounted to be a product of sound scholarship.

[42] The reference is possibly to Charles Sandoe Gilbert (1760–1831), son of Thomas Gilbert, and a historian of Cornwall. He wrote extensively on antiquity, heraldry and the genealogies of Cornwall. His works were illustrated by Henry Perlee Parker. The two large volumes he wrote on 'an Historical Survey of the County of Cornwall, to which is added a Complete Herald of the same, with Numerous Woodcuts', are still considered one of the best works on Cornwall.

and Murray[43]. I cannot say if a restless breeze occasionally ruffled the surface of this enforced calm. But in her deliberately anodyne life style, there was no chance of anything more substantial than a breeze which might cause her more mental turbulence than she could handle. In this situation, suddenly an impediment arrived in a motor-car, in the middle of the road, without any prior warning. All the weighty histories of Greece and Rome lightened in an instant. A deeply engaging present shook her to her very core and commanded imperatively, 'Awake!' In a moment Labanya was fully awake, and saw herself as she really was — not through her cognitive faculties but through pain.

---

[43]Hugh Murray (1779–1846), the younger son of Matthew Murray, was a geographer. In 1808, he wrote *Enquiries respecting the Characters of Nations*. His magnum opus was *Encyclopaedia of Geography, a Description of the Earth, physical, statistical, civil and political*, published in 1834.

Chapter 5
Striking up Acquaintance

*L*et us leave behind the debris of the past and return to the creativity of the present. Labanya left Amit in her study and went off to get Yogamaya. Inside the room, Amit sat like a bumblebee surrounded by the inner petals of a lotus. As his gaze alighted on objects, they mysteriously touched his mind and turned it pensive. When his eyes rested on the shelves, the study table, or on the works of English literature, it seemed to him that the books had come to life. Labanya's books, read by her, their pages turned by her, books that carried her constant thoughts throughout long days and nights, books that had been singled out by her bright glances, books that had lain in her lap in her absent-minded moods. He gave a start when he saw Donne's[44] collected poetical works on the table. While at Oxford, Amit used to hold forth on Donne's long poems and the poetry of his contemporaries. The two minds now touched, as they converged on this poetical imagination.

As indifferent days had shaded into indifferent nights, Amit's mind had become blurred, like the loosely wrapped, well-thumbed text book which had seen many years, and still had not escaped the clutch of a schoolmaster's hand. The coming day held no anticipation. It was unnecessary to welcome the present day with heart and soul.

Now, in an instant he was transported to a new planet where everything weighed less. Feet lifted off the floor while walking. Each moment eagerly moved towards some unimaginable chance. His body felt like a flute as a light breeze touched it. When daylight fell on him, the excitement it generated was akin to the tree's sap flowing through it and making flowers bloom. An old, dusty curtain was suddenly whipped off his mind and he could taste the extraordinary from the most mundane things. When Yogamaya softly entered the room, the very naturalness of that act struck Amit like a divine revelation in his highly receptive mood. He said reverentially to himself, 'Ah! This is not just any entry, it is an arrival!'

---

[44] John Donne was an English poet (1572–1631). He had lived through the reign of Elisabeth I, James I and died during the turbulent reign of Charles I. He was also an Anglican priest whose sermons were famous.

Though she was close to forty, age had not withered her. It had merely given her a becoming gravity. Her fair face was full, her hair cut very short after the manner of widows, her eyes were both smiling and maternal, her smile gentle. A thick blanket covered her from head to toe. She wore no shoes, her bare feet peeped out fair and beautiful. When Amit bent and touched her feet, a holy feeling coursed through his veins.

When the first introductions were over, Yogamaya began to reminisce: 'Your uncle, Amaresh, was the leading lawyer in our district, and had once saved us from going bankrupt in a legal dispute over property. He used to call me "Boudidi".'[45]

By now, Amit had recovered his poise and the use of his tongue: 'I'm his unworthy nephew. My uncle saved your property, while I damaged it. You had gained as his "boudidi", but you will suffer only losses as my "mashima".'[46]

Yogmaya inquired, 'You have a mother?'

Amit tried to look orphaned, but his natural, irrepressible merriment ruined any tragic effect his answer might have created, '"Had" is the operative word. But I also should have had a mashima.'

Yogamaya responded immediately to his impish humour, 'Baba[47], why this longing for a mashima?'

---

[45] Boudidi is a term used by younger brothers and sisters-in-law to address the elder brother's wife.

[46] Mashima is a term used to address mother's sister.

[47] Baba is a term of endearment used by older relatives to address young men.

Amit, having regained the full use of his eloquence, began the usual patter of words, 'Just imagine, had I smashed my mother's car, she would have scolded me endlessly. She would have said, it was a baboon's act. But if it was my mashima's car, she would indulgently smile at my ham-handedness, and dismiss it as "childishness".'

Yogmaya had to smile, 'Well then, let the car belong to your mashi.'

Amit leapt up and dived for Yogamaya's feet, 'For this very reason, one is compelled to believe in karma. I have only known a mother's lap, but had performed no rigid meditation for a mashi. The motor accident cannot by any stretch of the imagination fall under the category of good work! And yet, like a divine boon a mashima arrives in my life! Only the accumulation of many centuries of good karma can account for such strange good fortune.'

Amused, Yogamaya asked, 'Whose karmic gain, baba? Yours, mine, or the motor mechanic's?'

Amit, running his hands through his thick hair and thoughtfully considering the point, said, 'Tough question. An individual's good karma couldn't generate so much energy – the positive karma of the entire universe must have been converging for centuries – the flash point was the collision at 9.48 a.m. sharp! How's that?'

Yogamaya glanced sideways at Labanya and smiled a little. Within a few minutes of this new acquaintanceship, she was convinced that those two must marry. She set the promising ball rolling right away, 'Dears, chat together, get to know each other – I'll go and make arrangements for your lunch.'

Amit was supremely equipped to strike up fast-paced friendships and he wasted no time: 'Mashima has ordered us to know each other. Names come first. Let's tackle that requirement right now. You know my name, don't you? What the English grammar calls "proper name"?'

Labanya temporised, 'Well, I know you as Amit babu.'

Amit shook his head – 'That doesn't work everywhere.'

Labanya laughingly parried, 'There may be many situations – but the holder of a name normally owns just one.'

Amit dodged the logic adroitly, 'Your statement belongs to a previous age. It is unscientific to insist that, unlike the relativity of time, place and agency, nomenclature is fixed. I'm determined to propose the theory of the Relativity of Names to enter the halls of fame. As a start to realising this ambition, let me tell you that my name is not "Amit babu" as far as you are concerned.'

Labanya spiritedly entered into Amit's playful banter, 'Perhaps you prefer the English style? Mr Roy?'

Amit evaded getting verbally pinned once again. 'That's really unnervingly distant, with the seas stretching in between. To actually determine the right wavelength of a name, you should measure the time it takes to travel from the portals of the ear to the inner space of the heart.'

Labanya enquired curiously, 'So what's this fast-paced name?'

Amit answered readily, 'To increase velocity, mass has to be reduced. Delete babu from Amit.'

Labanya stalled a little before Amit's headlong entry into friendship, and shook her head, 'It isn't easy, it'll take time.'

But Amit remained unfazed at Labanya's response, 'Well, everybody shouldn't measure out time the same way. There is no such thing as one-watch, though there are pocket-watches – and they mark time according to the pockets they occupy. This is Einstein's theory.'

Labanya, however, disengaged herself from the conversation, stood up and said, 'The hot water for your wash is getting cold.'

Amit persisted, 'I will happily wash with cold-water, if you will stay and talk to me now.'

Labanya was smilingly firm in her refusal, 'There's no time, I've work to do.' With that, she left.

Amit did not immediately go for his wash. Instead he dwelt pleasurably on the conversation, the way Labanya had shaped each word with slight smiles. Amit had seen many beautiful girls, but their beauty resembled refulgent, yet shadowy, full-moon nights. Labanya's beauty was like the morning, there was no shadow-play; it was flooded with the clear light of intelligence. While fashioning her, the Creator had added a masculine element to her femininity. It was apparent at first glance that Labanya had not only the strength to bear pain, but also the ability for great mental exertions. It was this that had attracted Amit so powerfully. Amit himself had intelligence, but no ability to forgive. He was analytical, but lacked patience. He had learnt much, known much, but these mental attainments hadn't given him peace. He had seen in Labanya's face a profound peace, not the result of a full heart, but something that came from a decisive, deeply analytical intellect.

Chapter 6

Beyond Introductions

Amit's was a highly gregarious nature. The manifest beauties of nature could not hold his attention for long. His tongue normally ran on wheels, and in the forests and hills, he had very unresponsive listeners. They failed dismally to respond to witticisms. All his attempts at contrary behaviour boomeranged badly. The trees and the mountains moved according to set schedules, and expected others to respect their own schedules in equal measure. In a word, they were stolidly respectable. For this reason Amit, under ordinary circumstances, would have become tired of sylvan bliss and sighed longingly for the beckoning city lights.

Strangely enough, now the Shillong hills seemed to put out long invisible tentacles around Amit and pull him into their solidity. Today he had woken up before sunrise, totally contrary to his habitual hours. Beyond his window, he saw the delicate fringes of the Debdaru trees shivering slightly. Just behind them, the sun was drawing its golden fingers across the thin cloud cover over the mountains – and the fire-touched colours against the sky proudly defied all verbal descriptions.

Amit quickly swallowed a cup of tea and headed for the great outdoors. The road was deserted. He sat with legs outstretched on the thick, perfumed bed of pine-leaves, under a very ancient pine tree, heavily covered with moss, and lit a cigarette. The cigarette remained loosely held between two lazy fingers – the smoker had forgotten to smoke.

The forest lay alongside the road leading to Yogamaya's residence. Like an appreciative sniffer of appetising smells wafting from the kitchen just before a feast, Amit breathed in the pleasurable aroma of Yogamaya's house from this congenial spot. As soon as the hands of the clock pointed to a polite hour, Amit would hot-foot it there and demand a cup of tea. In the beginning, his appointed visiting hours were in the evening. But his reputation as a literature lover had earned him a round welcome at all hours of the day-ostensibly to discuss the finer points of literature. For the first couple of days, Yogamaya had been an enthusiastic participant, but it became quickly apparent to her that her presence dampened the other party. Since then, a spate of domestic duties began to demand Yogamaya's immediate presence. Her long absences from the interesting discussions, if carefully analysed, had to be ascribed, not to the inevitable chores, or even to fate, but as contrivances of her own ingenuity. She had correctly concluded that merely similar literary tastes could not account for the deeper note in these discussions. Amit also figured out quickly that his mashi's advanced years had not dimmed her observational powers, and her heart had remained tender. His zeal for further discussions grew keen under this surreptitious encouragement. To extend the appointed hour to its maximum extent, he entered into a pact with Jyotishankar, which bound him to help Jyoti with English literature for an hour in the mornings and for another two hours in the evenings. His help came in such huge quantities, along with so much airy persiflage, that the entire morning would slide into forenoon. Then, for both politeness' sake and at Yogamaya's request, he would stay back for lunch. The hours of duty, it was soon seen, kept increasing by the hour

Amit's educational mission for Jyoti's mental improvement was scheduled to start at eight every morning. When Amit had enjoyed a normal state of mind, he would have considered such an hour positively ungodly. He used to say, the sleep of a creature which had spent ten months in the womb could not and should not be patterned on that of the birds and the beasts. Amit's nights normally extended their sleep-laden touch on quite a few morning hours. In extenuation, he would remark that the stolen hours of sleep in the morning, precisely because they were stolen, were the most conducive for sound sleep.

Nowadays, his hours of blissful rest were cut short by his own innate yearnings. His eyes would open long before he wanted, but then, going back to sleep was unthinkable, in case he overslept. Occasionally, he had even advanced the hands of the clock, but since he did not want to get caught, he did not dare do it very frequently. Today, too, as his gaze rested on his watch, and its hands stood perversely on the wrong side of seven o'clock, he was convinced that it had stopped working. He brought it close to his ear, and heard its unmistakable ticking.

With a start he suddenly saw Labanya coming down the road, one hand swinging an umbrella. She was in a white sari, a triangular black shawl decorated with a black fringe was wrapped around her. Amit swiftly divined that Labanya had seen him in her peripheral vision, but was unwilling to turn it into a frontal gaze. Amit could not restrain himself anymore when she began rounding the corner without acknowledging his presence, but ran and caught up with her. He then said accusingly, 'You knew you couldn't avoid me, but you still made me run! I suppose you don't know how inconvenient it is when you get out of earshot?'

Labanya put on an innocent face, 'What's so inconvenient about it?'

Amit, with a comically woebegone expression, answered, 'The very soul of the wretched fellow who lags behind wants to yell out a particular name. But how am I to summon you? The gods and goddesses are easier to handle for they are happy to be invoked on a regular basis. Even if you roar out "Durga, Durga" at the top of your voice, Dasabhuja[48] is not displeased. The problem arises with you ladies.'

---

[48] Dashabhuja is another name for Durga, and means the Goddess with ten hands.

Lavanaya said mischievously, 'The problem is solved if you don't summon us.'

Amit returned immediately, 'I manage without any particular form of address when you are nearby. Which is why I say, don't go too far away. Being totally unable to call out just when I'm longing to do so is really the greatest of all tragedies.'

'Why, you know the western style of address,' teased Labanya.

Amit repudiated such a suggestion with vehemence, 'Miss Dutt? That can only be done at a tea-table! Look, when the earth met the sky at day-break today, they wanted to celebrate the moment of their mutual meeting with inspired new names that sweepingly included within their ambits both heaven and earth. Don't you think that a name is being called from on high and an answer from the ground is being breathed upwards? Wouldn't you say that similar moments are also possible when a new naming becomes an imperative need in the life of a human being? Just imagine! I have given you a full-throated call from my very heart right now! The sound of the name is reverberating through the forests, is travelling all the way up to those rosy clouds, and that mountain over there, when it hears the call, wraps its head up in a cloud, and thoughtfully stands still. Can you, by any stretch of your imagination, think of that name as "Miss Dutt"?'

Labanya avoided giving an answer to this fanciful and charged question, and said prosaically, 'It takes time to think of names. In the meanwhile, let's go for a walk.'

Amit kept her company, talking incessantly, 'Human beings learn to walk at a later stage, but with me it's just the opposite.

It is only now, after so many years, because I'm here that I've finally learnt how to sit. There is a proverb in English, "a rolling stone gathers no moss" – keeping that in mind, I've been sitting on the roadside long before day-break. And a good thing too. I managed to see the morning sun.'

Labanya hurriedly changed the subject. 'What's the name of that bird with the green wings?'

Amit said a little ruefully, 'I have always known as a general fact that in the world of living beings, there are also birds, but I have never bothered to know them particularly. Surprisingly, it is only after I've come here that I've noticed there *are* birds, and what's more, they also sing.'

Labanya broke into laughter, 'Very surprising!'

Amit was mock-serious, 'You're laughing! It's my pernicious habit to come out with the deepest insights frivolously. It's the effect of the moon presiding over the moment of my birth. It *has* to give a little smile even as it dies before the engulfing blackness of a moonless night.'

Labanya was still amused, 'Don't blame me. Even that bird over there would have laughed if it had heard you.'

Amit suddenly became serious. 'Folks don't immediately get what I say, so they laugh. If they understood, they would have remained thoughtfully silent. Today people are laughing at my confession that I have just come to know of birds. But the underlying truth is that today, I'm getting to know everything anew, even myself. This is beyond laughter. See for yourself – the words are still the same but you are now silent.'

Labanya smiled and said, 'You yourself are not too many days old, still pretty new, I should say, so why this whimsical search for more newness?'

Amit was now in dead earnest, 'There is no frivolous answer to this — nothing fit for the tea-table. The new wave sweeping over me is as old as time, as old as the dawn, as ancient as a bud blooming, just a new discovery of an eternal truth.'

Labanya did not say anything, just smiled.

By now Amit was in spate, 'This time your smile resembles the beam of a watchman's lantern focused on a thief. I know you've already read the original in the works of your favourite poet. For mercy's sake, don't put me down as a hardened thief. At times, the mind is impelled to become like Shankaracharya[49] — it asserts firmly the futility of claiming authorship when such dividing lines themselves are mere maya. Look, just this morning I had a sudden urge to find out a line from the literature I am familiar with, but which could have only come from my pen, no one else's.'

Labanya could not help asking, 'So, did you find it?'

Amit nodded, 'Yes, I have.'

Labanya's curiosity got the better of her and another question slipped out, 'Do tell me which one it is.'

---

[49] Shankaracharya was a great religious reformer and teacher of the Vedanta philosophy who lived in the 8th or 9th century AD. He was from the Malabar region, but he travelled extensively all over the sub-continent.

Amit said passionately, '"For God's sake hold your tongue and let me love".'

Labanya's heart trembled. After a long while, Amit asked again, 'I'm sure you know whose lines they are?'

Labanya inclined her head slightly, indicating assent.

'The line wouldn't ever have entered my head had I not discovered Donne on your table the other day,' Amit confessed.

Labanya asked, 'You discovered Donne?'

Amit was matter-of-fact, 'What else could it be? In a bookshop, one sees books, but on your table books reveal themselves. I have seen the tables in the public libraries – they bear books; your table gives them shelter. That day I saw Donne's poetry with my heart. It struck me that like beggars jostling for their share of charity at a rich man's wake, crowds also fight for elbow room at the doors of other poets. Donne's wide halls are quiet, offering enough space to two people to sit side by side. That's why I heard my morning's lines echoing the wish of my heart so clearly – "For God's sake, hold your tongue and let me love".'

As the lines were delivered in Bengali, Labanya was surprised, 'You write Bengali poetry?'

Amit was whimsical, 'I'm afraid I'll start writing poetry from today. The old Amit Rai has no clue to the new erratic Amit Rai. Maybe he will take it into his head to fight somebody.'

Labanya was startled, 'Fight? With whom?'

Amit was comically uncertain, 'I haven't decided that yet. I just feel I should shut my eyes and offer up my life for some really noble cause, and if I have to repent my decision, I can always do it after the deed is done.'

Labanya began to laugh, 'If you are bent on sacrificing your life, do it with due caution.'

Amit was sagacious, 'It is not necessary to tell me that. I refuse to get into any communal riot. I will move with great care, avoiding both the Muslims and the English. But if I spot some elderly fellow, a non-violent, pious type, driving along in a motor car and hooting away on the horn, I will stand in his way and yell, "Give battle!" The kind of man who avoids hospitals but comes here for a change of air to aid his digestion, and who brazenly takes the air to increase his appetite.'

Labanya laughed, 'What if the man refuses to obey you, and leaves?'

Amit declared solemnly, 'Oh, then standing well back, I'll raise both my arms to the sky and say, "I forgive you this time, you are like my brother, we are both sons of Mother India." I hope you understand that when the mind reaches an extremely elevated state, it is as easy to fight as it is to forgive.'

Labanya laughed again, 'I have to admit to some qualms while you were talking of fighting, but now that you have explained your policy of forgiveness, I am completely relieved.'

Amit ventured on a new line, 'Will you entertain a request?'

'What is it?' Labanya asked good humouredly

Amit said tentatively, 'Don't take a long walk to increase your appetite today.'

'Very well, what next?'

'Come, let's sit down there, under that tree, where there is a little rivulet flowing next to that mossy rock,' Amit said persuasively.

Labanya looked at her wrist-watch, 'But there really is very little time.'

Amit complained, 'That's the biggest tragedy of life, Labanya devi, there is no time. While travelling through the desert, one has just half a quart of water. One has to see that it does not spill into the dry sand and get unnecessarily wasted. Only those who have loads of time should have the luxury of being punctual. God has boundless time, so the sun rises and sets punctually. But as our time is short, if we waste time by being punctual, we are being just plain extravagant. If somebody from Amaravati asks us, "What did you do on earth?", should we say, "Well, we were so busy watching the clock, we did not have eyes for anything else."? Therefore I'm compelled to say, let's go and sit in that spot.'

If Amit had no objection to something, he couldn't imagine anybody else having any other view. For this very reason, it was difficult to reject his proposals. Labanya yielded, and said, 'Let's go.'

Thickly wooded shades. A narrow pathway descending to a Khasia village below. Halfway down this road, a thin rivulet, ignoring the man-made path, had cut its way independently next to it, and as a stamp of ownership, had strewn pebbles across it for good measure. The two sat down on a rock at this spot.

Just here, within a deep gorge, a pool of water seemed like a purdahnashin[50] girl, hidden behind a curtain of still green, afraid to step out of doors. The enveloping silence was so complete that Labanya felt strangely exposed. She wanted to say something to shake off the embarrassment gripping her. But she could not think of a single word, afflicted with the paralysed vocal chords of one's dreams.

Amit intuitively understood the necessity for a few words. He began, 'Look, Aryaa[51], we have two forms of language, formal and colloquial. But there should have been another form, not for society, not for business, but for such quiet, sequestered spots. It should have been as spontaneous as bird-songs, as poetry from a poet, it should have left our throats effortlessly, just like our weeping. To express themselves at such moments, if people have to run to bookshops, it would be a crying shame. Just imagine the problems we would have faced if people had to run to the dentist every time they felt like laughing. Be frank, Labanya devi, don't you feel like singing out your words?'

Labanya's head remained low and she was quiet.

---

[50] A woman who does not appear before strange men even in the private space of a residential house, but occupies a separate interiorised zone is called purdahnashin (within the curtain).

[51] Āryā, the feminine of Ārya, a term used to denote the pastoral groups who invaded India around the 7th century BC. There is an immense academic debate about the exact place of their origin, but it is generally held to be Central Asia.

Amit continued, 'At the tea-table, it is difficult to come to any conclusion about what is polite and what isn't. Here the question of rudeness or politeness doesn't arise. So what's to be done? To make our minds easy it is necessary to recite a poem. Prose takes a lot of time, and that kind of time we don't have. I can begin if you give permission.'

To refuse permission to cover embarrassment would have meant suffering even greater embarrassment, so Labanya, willy-nilly, gave permission.

As a start to his recitation, Amit challenged, 'I suppose you like Robi Thakur's poetry?'

'Yes, I do, Labanya said simply.

Amit declared, 'I don't. You'll have to excuse me. I have a particular poet, who writes so well he has very few readers. In fact, people don't even consider him to be important enough for abuse. I would like to recite from his poetry.'

'Why are you so apprehensive?' Labanya asked.

Amit explained, 'My experience has been pretty disheartening so far. If we criticise the poet, you ostracise us; if we try to silently ignore the man, it arouses even sterner reactions. All the bloodshed in the world is caused by someone disliking what someone else likes.'

'Don't expect me to become bloodthirsty. To justify my taste, I don't have to beg for someone else's encomium,' was Labanya's firm response.

Amit said approvingly, 'That's very well said. Right, then let me begin this fearlessly,

> *Hey Unknown, try escaping from my iron hold*
> *Till your depths I've not thoroughly known.'*

Breaking off, Amit held forth, 'Observe the subject – it's the bonding of not-knowing. We are imprisoned in an unknown world. Unless we know it, we cannot be free. This is the core of the theory of freedom.' He resumed his recitation:

> *'In a moment of blindness*
> *Hovering between sleep and wakefulness,*
> *When the night slides into dawn,*
> *Your face I suddenly saw.*
>
> *Eye to eye, demanded I,*
> *The location of your residence.*
> *Within my own amnesiac self do you hide from prying eyes?'*

Amit stopped here and again launched into his own views – 'The most obscure corner is your own forgotten self. We do not get to see the richest treasures enriching our lives because they are all hidden in this forgotten place. But that doesn't mean we have to give up.' So saying he again burst into poetry,

> *'To get to know you better,*
> *Won't be an easy matter.*
> *Certainly can't be done with soft murmurings in the ear.*

> *I'll win you over.*
> *Your voice, unconvinced, blurry with doubt,*
> *With firm strength I'll pull out*
> *From the grip of fear, shame, needless debate,*
> *Into the remorseless light of day.'*

Amit broke off again to give Labanya the benefit of his commentary, 'Sheer persistence. How very forceful. Observe the tremendous masculinity of the lines.' And Amit declaimed passionately,

> *'Bathed in tears you'll wake,*
> *And immediately be self-cognisant.*
> *Shedding the skin of ignorance*
> *In your freedom is my own freedom ordained.'*

'You won't get just this tone from your famous writer, this is like a fiery fury in the universe. It is not just lyrical, it is a cruel existential philosophy.' Then gazing at Labanya's face steadily, he recited softly,

> *'O Incognita,*
> *Days pass, the sun sets, time doesn't wait.*
> *A strong sudden gust,*
> *Snaps ties, severs bonds.*
> *The flames, revealing knowledge of you, burning bright,*
> *In reverential homage, as a gift I offer my life.'*

Almost before he had finished his recitation, Amit grasped Labanya's hand. Labanya did not pull it away. Wordlessly, she glanced at Amit's face.

After this, there was no need to say anything. Labanya even forgot to glance at her watch.

Chapter 7

Matchmaking

Amit came to Yogamaya and began on a wheedling note, 'Mashima, I've come with a marriage proposal. Don't be miserly and send me off.'

Yogamaya, rising instantly to the occasion, said teasingly, 'Absolutely no chance if I don't approve. First give me the patra's[52] name, residence and other particulars.'

It was difficult to discomfit Amit; his reply came promptly, 'The name doesn't even begin to indicate the patra's value.'

Yogamaya returned playfully, 'In that case, the matchmaker's fees will certainly be cut.'

---

[52]In this context Pātra signifies a bridegroom. It can also mean a vessel, or a person holding an important official post.

Amit retorted with spirit, 'This is totally unjust. A person with a big name has to spread himself very thin, a huge chunk of his investments are in the public zone, very little is invested at home. Instead of soothing ruffled feathers on the homefront, his time is taken up in furbishing up his public image. The wife gets a very meagre share of her husband, certainly not enough for a complete marriage. A public person's marriage is only a part-time marriage, as condemnable as polygamy.'

Yogamaya said, considering the matter, 'Well, never mind if the name falls a little short, what about looks?'

Amit said merrily, 'I can't give an opinion on that, I may exaggerate.'

Yogamaya said, tongue-in-cheek, 'Are you pushing it through the market on the strength of exaggerated claims?'

Amit of course had a ready reply, 'While selecting a patra two things must be kept in mind – the groom shouldn't outstrip the home by dint of his name, neither should he outstrip the bride by dint of his looks.'

Yogamaya was really enjoying this, 'Very well, leaving aside the questions of name and looks, what about the rest?'

'The remainder may be lumped together as 'worth'. Well, the man is not worthless.' Amit was irrepressibly impish.

Yogamaya inquired, 'Intelligence?'

'He has enough intelligence to delude people into thinking he is intelligent', Amit said disarmingly.

Yogamaya pushed the point relentlessly, 'Knowledge?'

Amit replied glibly, 'Like Newton's. He knows pretty well he has gathered only a few pebbles on the beach of the ocean of knowledge. But unlike Newton, he dare not say it out loud, just in case people believe him.'

'The patra's list of accomplishments seems pretty much on the short side', Yogamaya summed up.

'To reveal Annapurna in all her plenitude, Shiv feels no embarrassment in claiming a beggar's status,'[53] replied the undaunted Amit.

Yogamaya unbent a little, 'Be a bit clearer about the groom's identity.'

Amit said, 'Known family. The name of the groom is Amit Kumar Rai. Why are you laughing, Mashima? Do you think I'm joking?'

This time there was a thread of seriousness in Yogamaya's banter, 'Baba, I must confess I am a little nervous about your ability to turn it into a joke.'

Amit, however, was still lighthearted, 'This is a needless slur on the groom's character.'

Yogamaya relented, 'Baba, it's no mean ability to keep the weight of the world light with laughter.'

---

[53] Annapurnā literally means the goddess who bestows annam (rice). There is a Purānic narration about Shiva appearing before Annapurnā with a beggar's bowl, and Annapurnā, the beneficent form of Durgā, filling it.

Amit said, 'Mashi, only gods have that power and so they are unsuitable for marriage – Damayanti[54] knew about this.'

Yogamaya asked unexpectedly, 'Do you truly love my Labanya?'

Amit sensed the difference in tone and instantly responded earnestly, 'Just tell me how I should prove it.'

Yogamaya said a little cryptically, 'Its only test is for you to know with dead certainty that Labanya is really yours.'

Amit was a little baffled, 'Expound a little, please.'

Yogamaya gave a slight hint this time, 'Only that jeweller is astute who knows the true worth of a jewel even though he got it at a throw-away price.'

Amit tried to lead the conversation back into its previous lighthearted groove, 'Mashima, you're turning this into a very fine intellectual matter. It's almost as if you are polishing the psychological angles of a short story! It still remains fairly simple – in accordance with the laws of nature, a respectable young man is bent on marrying a respectable young woman as he loves her. The fellow, a mixture of good and bad, is quite passable, the young lady is above comment. In such a situation, normal mashimas,

---

[54]Damayanti, an early heroine in a *Mahabharata* narrative. She was a princess who married Nala, a king. Her choice was approved by her father. Through a series of domestic misfortunes, Nala and Damayanti were parted. But she remained faithfully constant and even managed to recognise her lord from six identical Nalas, five of whom were Devas and the last Nala.

driven by their natural affections, immediately get active on the dhenki[55] to prepare anandanadus[56].'

Yogamaya was affectionately reassuring, 'Don't worry, dear boy, my foot is already on the dhenki. Be assured that you've got Labanya. But only if your desire to get Labanya even after this certainty remains as intense, I'll know you're worthy of her.'

Amit was amazed, 'You've succeeded in stunning someone as modern as me.'

Yogamaya inquired, 'What signs of modernity have you observed?'

Amit was a little rueful, 'I see that twentieth century mashimas are scared even to give their wards in marriage'.

Yogamaya gravely gave the reason, 'The mashimas of the last century gave away in marriage girls who were mere dolls. The candidates for marriage today have no mind to satisfy their mashimas' desires for infantile games.'

Amit became eloquent in reply, 'Anxieties are unnecessary. Amit Rai has been born in this world just to prove that the desire to get someone doesn't end after they are formally united. In fact, desire increases in intensity precisely after such formal acknowledgements. He will demonstrate this by marrying Labanya. Otherwise, why should my car, though not sensitised to emotions, create such a strange accident in such a strange place at such a strange hour?'

---

[55] dhenki — husker
[56] Anandanadu, a sweet prepared specifically on ceremonial occasions. It is a mixture of jaggery and coconut.

'Baba, your tones don't reflect the gravity of someone mature enough to marry. I hope the entire thing does not become a farcical child marriage,' Yogamaya returned a little sharply.

Amit was comically contrite, 'Mashima, my mind has its own internal specific gravity, and it makes all my words, however grave, pop out of my mouth very lightly. But they are weighty for all that.'

Yogamaya went off to make arrangements for a feast. Amit restlessly drifted from room to room, but could not spot anyone special. Suddenly he came face to face with Jyotishankar, immediately recalling that that morning's session was bound over to *Antony and Cleopatra*.[57] Jyoti, scanning Amit's expressive face, realised he would have to make himself scarce out of sheer compassion for another human being. He asked accordingly, 'Amitda, I want to go on a trip to upper Shillong. Can I have the day off?'

Barely managing to contain his inner jubilation, Amit said expansively, 'Those who cannot take leave of their books now and then, are unable to process what they read. They only study mechanically. Why are you so needlessly apprehensive of my displeasure at such healthy attitudes?'

Jyoti said slyly, 'Tomorrow is Sunday, a holiday anyway, so I thought you might think…'

---

[57] William Shakespeare wrote the play *Antony and Cleopatra*.

Amit said hurriedly, 'I don't think like a schoolmaster, my friend. I don't consider routine holidays to be holidays. To enjoy a routine holiday is like hunting a shackled animal. It takes out the euphoric feel of a real holiday.'

Jyoti was hugely entertained by Amit's enthusiastic views on the theory of holidays, for Jyoti had divined the real reason for Amit's radical expositions on such themes. Now he teased, 'I've observed over the last few days your ideas on the subject of holidays are really breeding fast. Even the other day you offered me sage advice on the subject. At this rate, I will get to be an old hand at winkling out holidays from you.'

Amit, a little bemused, enquired, 'What advice did I give the other day?'

Jyoti was painstakingly and naughtily accurate, 'You said, "It is an important human virtue to have a sense of Irresponsibility. As soon as you hear its call, immediately obey its summons." The very next instant you glanced outside, shut your books and rushed out. The Irresponsible must have appeared in the vicinity, though it escaped my notice.'

Jyoti was twenty years old. His mind was just at the stage to get lightly rocked when it witnessed the deep restlessness which had seized Amit. So far he had relegated Labanya to the category of teachers. Today, Amit's experience had told him she belonged to the mysterious category of women.

Amit was back on balance, and laughingly replied, 'The market rates for advice like "Be prepared for work at any moment" are pretty high, just like the struck gold sovereigns of Akbar's. But on its flip side should be etched clearly another important maxim, "All Non-work should be welcomed with dauntless bravery".'

'We're getting treated to frequent samples of your dauntless bravery nowadays,' Jyoti returned wickedly.

Amit clapped Jyoti heartily on his back and prophesised, 'When the holy Ashtami[58] for sacrificing 'Important Work' appears in your calendar, don't waste a moment but immediately propitiate the goddess — Vijaya Dashami[59] advances on fleet feet and the goddess departs all too soon.'

Jyoti left. Though the sense of Irresponsibility was waiting for the summons, Non-work was taking its time to appear on the horizon. Amit wandered out of the house.

Blossom-laden creeper roses, sunflowers totally flooding one side, and the other side flaunting a chrysanthemum shrub in a square wooden tub. A huge eucalyptus tree grew at the upper end of a grassy slope. Sitting leaning against its trunk, with her legs outstretched, was Labanya. She had on an ash-grey shawl, and the morning sun slanted on her feet. On her lap, an out-spread handkerchief held some pieces of bread, and a few

---

[58] Ashtami / Mahashtami or the eighth day of the bright side of the moon, when the major worship of Devi Durga takes place. The length of the period of worship stretches over Sashti, Saptami, Ashtami, Nabami and Vijaya Dashami.

[59] Vijaya Dashami or the tenth day of the bright side of the moon, when the Devi prepares to depart.

broken walnuts. Her resolution of devoting the morning to the ministration of animals lay forgotten. Amit came and stood before Labanya and she glanced up and gazed at his face wordlessly, a gentle smile irradiating her own. Amit sat down in front of her, and said, 'I've got good news. Mashima has given her consent.'

Labanya threw a walnut fragment at a fruitless peach-tree without giving any answer. A squirrel came scurrying down its trunk. This creature happened to be one of Labanya's dependants.

Amit now said, 'If you've no objections, I'll trim your name a little.'

Labanya acquiesced, 'Trim it.'

'I will call you Bonyo.'[60]

'Bonyo!' Labanya was a little startled.

Amit said quickly, 'No, no, the name may blot your reputation. Such names fit only me. I'll call you – Bonya. What do you say?'

Labanya accepted without demur, 'Do so, but not before your Mashima.'

Amit agreed readily, 'Certainly not. These names are like secret mantras, and shouldn't be revealed to anybody. It is just for my lips and your ear.'

'Very well,' was the response.

---

[60]Bonyo – of the forest, metaphorically meaning wild or uncivilised.

Amit was enthusiastic, 'I also need an unofficial name like that. How about "Brahmaputra"? Bonya suddenly inundated its banks.'

Labanya was amused, 'It's a little too heavy for constant use.'

Amit agreed, 'You're right. We'll need a porter if we decide to use it. Why don't you give me a name? It'll have your creative stamp.'

'Right, then, I'll also trim your name. I'll call you Mita[61].' Amit was delighted, 'Wonderful! It has a companion in the Padabali[62] – *Bnadhu*. Bonya, on reflection, what's wrong in addressing me by this in front of others?'

Labanya replied gravely, 'I'm afraid its preciousness to a particular ear might be cheapened if more ears share its uniqueness.'

Amit was much struck, 'How true! What is a whole note between two pairs of ears, will get fragmented when many pairs strain to hear it. Bonya!'

'Yes Mita,' was the soft answer.

'Do you know which word I'll use to set your name to rhyme? Ananya.' Amit said impetuously.

'What will it signify?' Labanya was a little mystified.

'It'll mean that you are you, no one else,' Amit said in explanation.

'That's not particularly surprising,' Labanya observed.

---

[61] Mita or Mit – friend. 'Bnadhu' here means 'dear' and is a form of endearment.

[62] Padābali or lyrical poems sung by Vaishnavites. There are many major Vaishnav poets who composed padabalis.

Amit said forcefully, 'It's extremely surprising. It's a rare chance to come across a person who is just herself, and does not resemble others. My poem will emphasise this –

> O my Bonya, you're peerless,
> Incandescent in your true self, you're matchless.'

Labanya was amused, 'Are you going to take to writing poetry?'

'Of course I'll write poetry. Nobody can stop me,' Amit declared militantly.

'Why this sudden note of desperation?' Labanya was still amused.

'I'll give you a reason. Just like one tosses from side to side in bed if one can't get to sleep, I flipped back and forth through the entire Oxford Book of Verses till 2.30 last night. I just could not find a single love poem even though I used to trip over them before. I am sure the world is waiting for my poems to issue from my pen.' Amit announced and immediately seized Labanya's left hand in both of his, and continued, 'Now that both my hands are locked, how will I hold my pen? Two hands meeting rhyme the best. Which poet can write of something so elementary as your fingers talking to mine?'

'Nothing pleases you easily, Mita, and that's why I fear you so much.'

Amit insisted, 'But try to understand what I'm saying. Ramachandra wanted proof of Sita's truth with an externalised fire; and he lost her. Even the test of a poem is through an ordeal by fire, but it has to be the fire of the soul. A person who doesn't burn from within cannot test any poetical truth. He has to listen to the opinion of others, which are generally pretty slanderous. Today my mind has been fired, and I'm re-reading all that I've read so far – very little survives this fiery examination. They are all turning to ashes in the roaring flames. In the noisy assemblage of the poets, I have to stand up and say, 'Don't shout so much, just say the right thing softly –

> *For God's sake, hold your tongue*
> *And let me love!'*

The two sat still and wordless for a long while. Then after some time Amit picked up Labanya's hand and passed it over his face. Then he said wonderingly, 'Just think Bonya, there must be countless people in the world this morning, at this very moment, desiring something with every fibre of their being, and how very few actually get what they wanted. I am one of those very few. You are the only one in the whole wide world who can actually see that lucky man under an eucalyptus tree in the hills of Shillong. The most remarkable things in this world happen so silently they remain invisible. And yet your Tarini Talapatra can raise his fist to the sky and mouth the empty bombast of crooked politics! What's more, he will be heard from Goldighi in Calcutta to Noakhali-Chatgna! That abominable piece of bad news becomes something big in Bengal! Who knows, maybe it's for the best.'

Labanya asked, 'Which is for the best?'

Amit answered, 'It's good that the best things in this world actually roam around in full public view, and yet do not keep tripping over the avid gaze of the vulgar. Its deeper knowledge is tuned into the pulse beat of the universe. But Bonya, I'm talking my head off and you are sitting quietly — what are you thinking of?'

Labanya sat with downcast eyes and did not immediately answer.

Amit said again, 'Your silence dismisses my words like service terminated without any pay.'

Labanya, still with downcast eyes, said, 'You scare me with your words, Mita.'

Amit was surprised, 'What scares you ?'

Labanya said mournfully, 'You desire so many things from me, but I can't imagine how I can even give you a fraction of what you want.'

Amit waved aside Labanya's apprehensions, 'The value of your gift is precisely because you give so effortlessly, without even thinking about it.'

Labanya put her fears into words, 'When you said Kartama had consented, my heart felt a leaden sense of foreboding. I suddenly felt that the time for getting caught was drawing close.'

Amit said exultingly, 'But you *have* to get caught.'

Now Labanya abandoned her hesitant manner and said clearly, 'Mita, both your taste and your intelligence are far above mine. One day I will fall far behind you while we are walking through life together, and you won't turn around to hail me. I will not blame you one little jot then – no, no! don't say a word, hear me out first. Don't say you want to marry me, I beg of you. The more you try to untie the bonds of wedlock, the more tangled it gets. What I've received from you is more than sufficient for me, and it will certainly last through my lifespan. But you shouldn't delude yourself.'

Amit protested, 'Bonya, why are you raising the spectre of the possibility of miserliness in some tomorrow when today's generosity is so overwhelmingly real?'

Labanya said relentlessly, 'Mita, you have given me the strength to speak the truth. Deep within yourself, you know my words do ring true. You just won't own it in case the magic of the present moment is even slightly spoiled. You are not the person to revel in domesticity. You roam restlessly seeking something which will slake your aesthetic thirst. That's why you flit through works of literature so hungrily, and you seek me out precisely for this reason. Dare I say it? In your heart of hearts, you know the married state to be – vulgar, to use your own words. It's too respectable. It is the tame, sanctified-by-the-*Shastras* property of smug materialists who like to lean against fat cushions as they successfully conjoin worldly wealth with wife.'

Amit was startled by such cutting insights. 'Bonya, you can say the most astoundingly hard things in the most amazingly gentle voice.'

Labanya said tenderly, 'Mita, I hope I can always remain this hard, just on the strength of my love, and never ever attempt to cheat you by deluding you. Just be what you are, let whatever you like about me appeal to you, just as your taste dictates. But don't burden yourself with any responsibility. With that I'll be happy.'

Amit was uncharacteristically serious. 'Bonya, now let me have my say. You've certainly sliced open my character with amazing skill. I won't waste words arguing about it. But you've made one very serious mistake. A man's character also has movement. In its chained-up state, it is static, and totally domesticated. Suddenly, if fortune strikes a timely blow at its chains, it heads for the forests, and its very nature changes.'

Labanya had to ask, 'Which definition describes you today?'

Amit replied with deep feeling, 'Today I am that which is not the habitual me. I have struck up acquaintanceships with many girls before this, strictly within societal channels, on its ordered banks, under the shuttered lantern-light of taste. Here one just gets to see, but doesn't come to know. Tell me yourself, Bonya, do you and I share only that level of acquaintanceship?'

Labanya was silent.

Amit began to enthuse, as was his wont, 'Two planets move side by side in their fixed orbits, nodding to each other now and then in their politest manner. Their styles exude good manners and a safe distance, as if they keep in step because taste demands it, not because of the wild clamouring of their hearts. But if their paths cross in a fatal collision, their individual lights are put out by an all-consuming fire. That fire flared within Amit Rai and he had to change. Human history is like this. Though it resembles an inevitable succession of events, it is actually a string of sudden contingencies. Creation itself moves with sudden jerks, shoved periodically by suddenness itself, while centuries move to this uneven beat. You've changed my rhythm, Bonya, and my new rhythm can harmoniously contain both our tunes.'

Labanya's eyes filled with tears, but involuntarily she thought, Amit is basically a writer. When he confronts life, words come more naturally than emotions. Words are what he wants to harvest, what gives him joy. He needs me for the mass of frozen words weighing heavy on his mind. So far he has not been able to voice them. He wants my warmth to melt them, loosen them, and set them free.

The two sat quietly for a long time. Labanya suddenly broke the silence with a question, 'Well, Mita, has it ever struck you that Shahjehan was joyous about Mumtaz's death the day Taj Mahal finally stood completed? To realise his dream, her death was necessary. Mumtaz's greatest gift of love was her own death. The Taj Mahal does not reveal a grieving Shahjehan, it's actually an embodiment of his joy.'

An idea always excited Amit and he exclaimed, 'Your words give me thrilling jolts every second. You must be a poet.'

Labanya said firmly, 'I don't want to be a poet.'

'Why not?' Amit demanded.

Labanya's voice rang with conviction, 'I just don't want to light verbal lamps with this wonderful warmth of life. Words are for those who have been invited to light the festive lamps celebrating this world's existence. I'll reserve the warmth of life coursing through me for life's demand for action.'

Amit's animated protest reverberated with his own conviction, 'Bonya, you're denying the power of words? Aren't you aware of your words stirring me to my core? How should you know what you say, and the meanings your words assume in my mind! I see I have to summon Nibaran Chakraborty to my aid, even though you must be really fed up with his name by now. I'm tied by my heels to that fellow, as he is the treasurer of the words that bubble away in my head. Nibaran can still surprise himself, staleness has not as yet touched him. Every time he writes a poem, he writes it for the first time. I was leafing through his notebook the other day and I found a fairly recent piece. He seems to have divined my discovery of my fountain, here, in the Shillong hills, and in response he writes,

> *Fountain, in your crystal clear stream,*
> *The sun and the stars see their reflections beam.*

Had I been the poet, I couldn't have described you with greater clarity. You have this transparent quality about you that catches and reflects all the light radiating from the sky. I see the clear, reflected light in everything that characterises you – in your face, in your smile, in your words, when you sit still, when you walk on the road.

> *Today, by the wayside,*
> *Do meet my shadow in a dance,*
> *Your laughter mingling with its delight*

> *In sweet, harmonious strains.*
> *Give it the words of felicity,*
> *That belongs to you eternally.*

You are a waterfall, you don't merely move to life's current, but your words flow with your movement. As you rush along, you draw out music from even the hard, unresponsive stones. And then their song chimes out in joy.

> *My shadow and your laughter*
> *In sheer joyousness do merge.*
> *My poet within, at such blending,*
> *Sings out in verse.*
> *With your flashing light at every step,*
> *Words surge to my heart every moment.*
> *Today, in wondering delight I beheld,*
> *My very speech embodied in your cascade.*
> *My mind awakens at your flow,*
> *And myself I come to know.'*

Labanya smiled a little wanly and said, 'I may possess enormous quantities of light and equal amounts of sound, but that won't turn your shadow into substance. I won't be able to hold it fast.'

Amit said, 'But, then, even if I'm not present, you'll find my embodied speech.'

Suddenly Labanya smiled and asked, 'Where? In Nibaran Chakraborty's notebook?'

Amit grinned, 'I wouldn't be surprised. The hidden stream flowing under my heart seems to somehow erupt out of Nibaran's fountain.'

Labanya said lightly, 'Then perhaps I'll find your mind ensconced only in Nibaran Chakraborty's fountain one day, and nowhere else.'

Just then they were summoned to lunch.

As Amit walked down to the house, he pondered, 'Labanya wants to see everything clearly in the light of her intelligence. Even where human beings tend to delude themselves, she refuses to do so. I really cannot object to what she said a while back. Our lives have to give external shape to that deep intuition which our inner selves have felt – some do it through action, some do it through creativity. Creativity always touches life, but also moves away from it, like a river that cuts its banks and continuously moves away from them. Am I also fated to be swept along in the current of creativity and so move away from life itself? Is this the real difference between men and women? Man concentrates his last drop of energy to create. That same creativity, just to make its new form exist, has to forget its previous form. Woman uses her whole energy to conserve, and so stands in opposition to the new forms of creativity, just to protect the old. Creativity is cruel towards preservation; preservation opposes creativity as an obstacle. Why is it like this? At one point these two elemental forces will clash against each other. It is strange to be so akin and yet so very oppositional. Maybe the greatest gift for the two of us is actually freedom, not union.'

The thought wrenched Amit's heart, but his mind just couldn't ignore this unpleasant realisation.

Chapter 8

Labanya's Debate

Yogamaya asked, with a little hint of urgency, 'Ma Labanya, are you sure you've understood correctly?'

There was quiet certitude in Labanya's answer, 'Indeed I have, Ma.'

Yogamaya's voice was full of maternal love, anxiety, and excuses, 'I know Amit is very wayward. That's why I'm so very fond of him. Haven't you noticed how completely disorganised he is? It's like everything just slips away from him!'

Labanya gave a little smile as she said, 'He would stand in grave danger, if things didn't keep slipping away from him and he was compelled to hang onto things. His personality is such that either he will not really get what he's got, or, as soon as he gets it, he will lose it. His nature would rebel against hoarding carefully anything he has received.'

Yogamaya said fondly, 'Really, my dear, I find his childishness very endearing.'

Labanya was half-ironic, 'That's a mother's prerogative. Mothers are responsible for their offsprings' childishness. For all mothers, their sons are forever only playful. But why are you asking me to load someone with the kind of responsibilities he's just not equipped to bear?'

Yogamaya didn't allow Labanya's gentle remonstrance to weigh with her, 'Haven't you observed Labanya, even his volatile mind has become a lot quieter nowadays? It really pulls at my heartstrings to see him so subdued. Whatever you may say, he certainly loves you.'

Labanya agreed without any hint of coquetry, 'Yes, he does.'

Yogamaya said simply, 'Then stop worrying.'

Labanya said with great intensity, 'Kartama, I'm unwilling to inflict even the smallest torment on his basic nature.'

Yogamaya said a shade pleadingly, 'Labanya, as far as I've understood it, love desires to be tormented a little, to torment a little in return.'

Labanya replied patiently, but firmly, 'Kartama, that sort of torment is practiced in a different domain. But a person's basic nature can find it unbearable. It has repeatedly occurred to me, when I've read about love in literature, that love becomes a tragedy when human beings, even while recognising each other's need for independence, have refused to be content with this realisation. They have tried to remould, recreate each other in the way they desire, they have forcibly wanted to graft their own desires onto someone else.'

Yogamaya said persuasively, 'But, Ma, when two youngsters desire to settle down, each has to creatively remould the other to a certain extent – otherwise their new-found domesticity will be completely paralysed. Where there is love, this reinvention of each other is easy. Where there is none, and a hammer takes its place, what you call "tragedy" is sure to occur.'

Labanya's steely intellect flashed in her blistering answer, 'People who are made for domesticity can be left out of the discussion. They are soft clay, children of the earth, who, under the pressure of everyday-domesticity are remoulded naturally on the turning wheel – they won't resist. But persons who aren't soft clay, cannot at any point give up their individualistic, independent personalities. The woman incapable of understanding this, will become increasingly deprived even as her demands become more and more strident. The man who cannot understand this, and yet tries to enforce his will, simply loses the real person. I firmly believe that what we consider normally as "getting", is nothing more than a hand acquiring a hand-cuff.'

Yogamaya abandoned this particular line of argument and asked instead, 'Labanya, what do you want to do?'

Labanya said clearly, 'I don't want to marry him and make him miserable. Marriage isn't for everybody. You know, Kartama, there are fussy minds, and they selectively like certain qualities about other human beings. But netted in a marriage, men and women come suddenly very close to each other, and there is no space in between – the entire human being has to be reckoned with from very close quarters. There is no way one can keep even a part hidden.'

Yogamaya was again moved to protest, 'Labanya, you don't know yourself. There'll be no need to discard any part of you.'

Labanya refused to be swayed, 'But, he doesn't want me. I certainly don't think he has even seen the Labanya who is ordinary, homely. As soon as I touched his mind, it just exploded in this blaze of endless words. And he constructed me from these words. If his mind tires, his words dry up, he'll suddenly see me for what I am – an ordinary girl, who is not his creation. In a marriage, one has to adjust to the entire person, there is no more space to create an image.'

Yogamaya was a little disbelieving, 'You think Amit won't be able to adjust totally to even a girl like you?'

Labanya was a little wistful, 'If his nature changes, he'll be able to. But then why should he change! That's not what I want.'

Yogamaya asked a little sharply, 'What do you want?'

In Labanya's reply there was both sadness and philosophical acceptance, 'Till I can do so, I'll merge my self with his words, blend like a dream in the shadow-play of his mind. Anyway, why should I call it a dream? It's a particular birth of me, a particular form of me; it's true in a particular context. Let it be a newly-emerged, colourful butterfly, entitled to only a few days in the world – where's the harm – it's still real for all that.

Does it matter if it sees the light of the day at sunrise and dies at sunset? One should just make sure that the little time it has isn't wasted.'

Yogamaya was exasperated, 'All right, as I understand it, even if you were to remain like a temporary illusion in Amit's mind, it doesn't answer one question. What about you? Do you also wish to remain unmarried? Is Amit an illusion in your mind as well?' Labanya didn't answer, just sat quietly.

Yogamaya continued, 'When you argue, I can perceive you've read a lot of books. I cannot think like you, neither can I talk like you. Maybe, I cannot be as firm as you in action as well. But, Ma, I've caught glimpses of you beyond these arguments. It was roughly twelve at night – I saw your light was on. When I went to your room I saw you weeping on your table, your face between your hands. This is not a girl trained in philosophy. First I thought of going in to comfort you – then I felt that all girls will have to bear their share of weeping when its time to weep, any dilution of this pain doesn't have any meaning. I know very well that you want to love, you don't want to create. How will you live if you cannot burn in service? I shall have to say it – without him next to you, you'll be unfulfilled. So don't suddenly vow not to marry. I know how stubborn you can be once you've made up your mind, and it makes me anxious.'

Labanya remained silent, her face bent over hands engaged unnecessarily in pleating her sari-end on her lap. Yogamaya went on, 'Having observed you, I've often felt that you girls have developed extremely fine analytical minds capable of deep thoughts, but unsuitable for the crudities of our material conditions. The lights which had remained invisible to our untutored eyes are visible to your searching gazes. Such sophisticated thinking can transcend our very embodiedness. But even with our cruder intellects and perceptions of our times, we had our share of joy and sorrow. Nor could we avoid problems. But you lot are making everything so very complicated that nothing remains simple anymore.'

Labanya couldn't help smiling a little at that. Only the other day Amit had been lecturing Yogamaya on the concept of invisible light, and here it was, marching into Yogamaya's argument. As a concept, this, too, was refined, and would have been quite beyond Yogamaya's respected mother.

Labanya replied steadily, 'Kartama, as the passage of time teaches human beings to understand more, it also endows them with the strength to bear up under its weight. The fears and sorrows of darkness are unbearable, for they cannot be seen.'

Now Yogamaya said a little sadly, 'It would have been far better, I think, if the two of you had never met.'

The ever-calm Labanya suddenly broke down, 'No, no, no, never that, don't say that! I can't think of anything but this happening! I used to be so convinced that I had dried up – that I would only read books and pass examinations till the end of my days! Today, I'm suddenly aware that I, too, can love! It's much more than enough to know that such an impossibility has become a possibility in my life. I sometimes think I was nothing more than a shadow, and now I'm real. I don't want anything more. Don't tell me to marry, Kartama!'

So saying, Labanya left the couch for the floor and for Yogamaya's lap, where she burst into tears.

Chapter 9

Change of Residence

In the beginning, everyone was totally convinced that Amit would return to civilisation within a fortnight of his self-imposed exile. In fact, Noren Mittir had betted pretty heavily on its being even less than a week. One month passed, then two months. Still there was no news of the expected return. The contract for the hired house in Shillong had expired, some zamindar from Rangpur now sat there in occupancy. After a long search, a small place was found near Yogamaya's residence. Originally it had belonged to some mali or gowala[63]. It had then been taken over and given some touches of lower-middle class

---

[63]Mali, the caste name for gardeners. Gowala, the caste name for cowherds. Both are low in the caste hierarchy.

respectability by a poor clerk. That clerk too had died, and now his widow had taken to renting it out. Due to a paucity of doors and windows, the three elements – light, wind and the sky – were in very short supply. This lack was more than made up by that other element, rainwater – which descended in vast quantities through unseen cracks in the roof.

One day Yogamaya came to visit and exclaimed in horrified accents, 'Dear child, is this some kind of self-experimentation?'

Amit, insouciant as ever, replied airily, 'Uma[64] had meditated in a foodless state, and had even given up eating leaves towards the finish. My meditation is in a furniture-less state – I've given up beds, couches, tables, armchairs, and have at the moment reached the sublime state of retaining these bare walls. That effort had occurred in the Himalayas, this effort is occurring in the Shillong hills. On that occasion, the maiden had desired the groom, on this occasion, the groom desires the maiden. There, Narod[65] was the matchmaker, here there is Mashima herself. If Kalidasa can't make it here on time[66], then I suppose I shall have to take over his job as well.'

Amit had laughed while rattling off his spiel, but his words hurt Yogamaya's tender heart. She almost invited Amit to come

---

[64] Uma, the daughter of Himavat and the wife of Shiva.

[65] Narod, one of the saptarshis and also a dovotee of lord Vishnu. He has the reputation of being a mischief-maker.

[66] *Kumarasambhavam* is one of Kalidasa's major dramas, and narrates the birth of Kartikeya.

and stay with them, but stopped herself just in time. She thought to herself, half humorously, half grimly, that the Fates had cooked up something very complicated, and if we take a hand in it as well, the ensuing tangle might be past unravelling. She did, however, send some things over to make Amit a trifle comfortable, while her already deep affection for this feckless, wayward young man doubled in volume. She began to constantly tell Labanya, 'Ma Labanya, don't turn your heart into stone.'

One day, after a very heavy downpour, Yogamaya visited Amit's ramshackle little house to see how he was faring. She walked in to see Amit sitting under a rickety old table on a blanket, happily reading an English book. He had observed the uninvited arrival of rain within his room, and acting on a happy thought, had retreated with a blanket under the table, which he turned into a temporary cave. First he had enjoyed a good laugh by himself, and then lost himself in poetry. His mind, initially, had leapt towards Yogamaya's house, but his unprepared body stood in the way. In Calcutta, where it was never needed, Amit had bought a very expensive raincoat! It hadn't even occurred to him to bring it here, where it was constantly needed! He did possess an umbrella, which was either lying forgotten in the last place he had visited, or was still resting under the old deodar tree. Yogamaya was shocked as she took in this scene, 'Amit, *what's* all this?'

Amit quickly came out from under the table, and said light-heartedly, 'My room is suffering from unrelated delirium today, its condition isn't much better than mine.'

Yogamaya was temporarily diverted, 'Unrelated delirium?'

Amit explained, 'Meaning, this roof can almost be called Bharatvarsha. The relations amongst its various parts are tenuous. Therefore, as soon as there is trouble overhead, floods of tears begin raining from all directions, and if the storm hits the outer walls, the whole house begins to heave huge, shuddering sighs. As a sign of protest, I've put up a platform over my head, a good example of Home Rule in the face of such rank misgovernment within the room. The political moral is clearly discernible.'

Yogamaya felt amusement stir despite her deep concern, 'So what's this political moral?'

Amit said, deliberately infusing his words with an innuendo, 'The moral is that however powerful the house-owner may be, if s/he does not live in it, then the poor tenant's makeshift arrangements are far superior to such distant, impersonal rule.'

Today Yogamaya felt very angry with Labanya. The fonder she grew of Amit, higher and higher grew her opinion of him. In her mind, now he had assumed the very acme of perfection – 'So much knowledge, such intelligence, so many degrees, and yet so simple! What singular capacity to put wonderful thoughts in words! And if you were to speak of looks, then to my mind, Amit is much better looking than Labanya. Labanya is fortunate in that Amit, a prey to some peculiar planetary configuration, has become infatuated with her! And Labanya is causing such a perfect specimen of young manhood so much misery! She declares for no reason at all, she won't marry. Like some exalted queen! A vow for the broken bow![67] She'll come to grief for such arrogance! The stupid girl will have to weep for the rest of her life!'

Yogamaya's first instinct was to take Amit home with her in the car. But on second thoughts, she told Amit, 'Just wait here for a while, Baba. I'll come back soon.'

As soon as she reached home, she saw Labanya comfortably curled up on the sofa, a shawl on her feet, reading Gorky's *Mother*.[68] Her temper flared up at the sight of such callous enjoyment of comfort.

She said, 'Come, let's go for an outing.'

Labanya said wearily, 'Kartama, I don't feel like going out today.'

The idea that perhaps Labanya had run to the book and taken refuge in it only to escape from herself eluded Yogamaya. The entire afternoon Labanya had been poised on the brink of a restless expectation — the expectation of Amit's arrival. Her heart had been continually whispering, 'There he is.' The pine trees twisted every now and then under the lash of the wild, furious wind. The newly-born waterfalls were incessantly active

---

[67] In the *Ramayana*, written by the sage Valmiki, King Janaka had set a condition on the occasion of Sita's swayamvara. Shiva's bow, which Shiva had given to him, had to be strung in the open assembly.

[68] Maxim Gorky, 1868–1936, pseudonym of Aleksey Maksimovich Peshkov, a Russian short-story writer and novelist who first attracted attention with his naturalistic and sympathetic stories of tramps and social outcasts and later wrote other stories, novels, and plays, including his famous *The Lower Depths*.

under the torrential rain, almost as if they were racing against their short lifespan on these hills. One desire, reiterating itself over and over, grew stronger in Labanya's heart, making it restless – 'Today let all barriers break, all doubts fly away on swift wings, let me grasp Amit's hands and finally say, "I'm yours, for ever, through the ages."' Today saying it would be so easy. Today the entire sky was gripped by some strange desperation, booming out urgent messages. The far-flung forests, picking up its speech, were yelling out similar words. The rain-drenched mountain ranges were standing still with their ears attentively tuned in to the sky's voice. Let someone come to hear Labanya's words with such generous attention, such stillness, with such quiet greatness. But hour after hour went by, nobody came. The perfect time for saying what was in her heart was sliding away so fast! Even if someone did come after this moment had fled, the right words would falter and fail, all the doubts would come flooding back, for by then the tumultuous tandava[69] of the heavens would have faded away into the distance. Year after year silently passed by, and only for a brief spell, at a specially appointed hour, did speech unexpectedly knock at one's door. If one failed to find the doorkey, then the words lost their divine power, the right words remained unuttered. The day that speech came to call, one yearned to hail the whole world to give them the momentous news – 'Listen, everybody, I do love!' Like the migratory birds

---

[9]Tandava, the cosmic dance of Shiva.

coming from afar, the words, 'I do love' have travelled far, over vast distances. 'For these words, the god within my soul was ever vigilant. The instant these words touched me this day, my whole life, my whole world, flared into life.' Today, hiding her face in her pillow, Labanya kept telling someone, 'It's real, true, nothing can be as true as this.'

But the time for such a declaration elapsed, the much awaited guest didn't arrive. The leaden heaviness of empty waiting was making Labanya's heart ache, she went to the verandah and allowed the spray of the rain to soothe her. Then a huge tidal wave of hopelessness engulfed her heart; she began to feel that all the light in her life had blazed up for one glorious moment and then gone out, leaving nothing before her. All her courage to declare before Amit, her love for him, simply oozed out of her. The huge hope, which had buoyed her up a little while back, vanished, leaving her very tired. She remained still a long while and then finally pulled a book towards her from the table. It took some time to be able to concentrate, but as the words pulled her into the book, she unconsciously managed to forget herself.

Around this time, Yogamaya asked her to accompany her for a brief outing, and she could not summon up the requisite enthusiasm.

Yogamaya pulled up a seat and sat down before Labanya, fixed her with an angry glance and said sternly, 'Labanya, come, let me hear the truth, do you love Amit?'

Labanya hurriedly sat up and asked anxiously, 'Why do you ask me such a question, Kartama?'

Yogamaya said angrily, 'If you can't love him, why can't you tell him so plainly? You would be cruel to hold on to him without wanting him.'

Labanya's heart swelled with great emotion, she could not utter a word.

Yogamaya, unaware of Labanya's overwrought emotions, continued in the same vein, 'My heart broke when I went in a little while back and witnessed the state he is in. For whom is he spending his time here like a wretched beggar? Can you even begin to comprehend how fortunate any girl would feel when a boy like him wants her?'

With a great effort, Labanya forced her voice past the lump in her throat, 'You are asking me about my love, Kartama? I don't think there is anybody in this world who can love as I do! I can die for my love. All that I had till now has been totally consumed by it. This is a brand-new beginning for me, this love's beginning has no end. It is beyond my capacity to express this astounding feeling within the core of my being. Can anyone ever understand love the way I have understood it ?'

Yogamaya was amazed. She had always seen Labanya's calm content, this great torrent of surging emotions was indeed unimagined hidden depths. She said very gently, 'Ma Labanya, do not keep yourself enshrouded. Amit is searching for you in the dark — don't be afraid to reveal yourself completely to him. If he could see the light glowing within you, there would be no lack in his life. Come, Ma, come with me right now.'

The two went to Amit's cottage.

Chapter 10

The Second Sadhana

Amit was seated on a pile of newspapers he had spread out on the damp couch. On the table a sheaf of foolscap paper bore witness to Amit's preoccupation with writing. In fact, it was around this time that he had decided to pen his autobiography. The reason, as he explained it, was his sudden vision of his life in kaleidoscopic colours, like the rain-washed Shillong hills gleaming freshly on a new day. He had understood the value of his own existence, so how could he restrain himself from self-expression? Amit had his own opinion as to why biographies of people were written after their deaths. In his words, it was only after dying in the material world, that people came to life within others' hearts. Amit applied the analogy to his own experience. He had died in a material sense during his sojourn in the Shillong hills. His past had vanished like a mirage, and in a different sense, he had been reborn with a keen appreciation of life. His new life stood etched in incandescent lines against the dark background of his forgotten past. This revelation had to be recorded. For, there were very few people in the world who underwent this experience. Normally, from birth to death, they lived in the twilight zone of a half-life, like bats in dark caves.

It was still raining a little. The gusty wind had died, the clouds had become lighter.

Amit sprang from the couch, and complained, 'This is really wrong, Mashima.'

Yogamaya, indulgent as ever of Amit's moods, asked, 'Why, Baba, what have I done?'

Amit said unhappily, 'I'm totally unprepared. What will Shrimati Labanya think?'

'It's necessary to make Shrimati Labanya think a little. One should know all there is to know. So why is Shriyukta Amit so apprehensive about this?'

'Shrimati Labanya should know all that there is to know about Shriyukta's glorious wealth. To convey the wants of the Shriheen, the poverty-stricken, there's you, my very own mashima,' said Amit, with a touching blend of pride and trust.

'Why such differentiation, Baba?' Yogamaya asked quizzically.

'In sheer self-interest,' returned Amit. 'One should claim glorious wealth with glorious wealth, and by displaying one's lack, ask for blessings. The Labanya devis throughout human civilisation have aroused a soul-stirring realisation of glory, and the mashimas have showered blessings.'

Yogamaya stated, 'It's possible to have both the devi and the mashima; there is no need to cover any lack.'

Amit emitted a shower of words in response, 'Only poetry can reply to this. Whatever I say in prose I need to clarify by taking recourse to rhyme. Matthew Arnold has called poetry "criticism of life", I want to modify it a little by calling it "life's commentary in verse". I'm informing the special guest well in advance that whatever I'm going to read out, has not been written by any Emperor of Verse –

> *What needs a full heart to demand,*
> *Don't beg for with an empty hand,*
> *Don't approach the door with eyes wet and wan.*

If you think about it, love is wholeness, its desires are not akin to the begging of the poor. When the gods love their devotees, only then they approach the devotee's door for alms.

> *When necklaces past price you get*
> *Exchange of garlands then expect.*
> *Your devi's seat don't spread out*
> *On the side of the dusty, lowly road.*

That's why I recently requested the devi to reconsider her options before she entered the room. I can't spread out anything for her as there is nothing to spread – merely these wet newspapers. Nowadays, I really fear editorial ink-marks the most. The poet exhorts us to hail the person we want when the cup of life is brimming over, but not to share in our thirst.

> *In the flowery, vernal spring*
> *Clasp close your constant treasure trove,*
> *When a million lamps with tongues of flame*
> *Dispel darkness in a golden blaze.*

In the laps of the mashis human beings begin their first meditation for realising the truth of poverty – the naked sannyasi's search for affection. In this little cottage, all its harsh prerequisites have been met. I am determined to call this hut 'Mastuto[70] Bungalow.'

Yogamaya responded maternally to this quixotic mixture of philosophy and nonsense, 'Baba, the second meditation is for the realisation of glorious wealth, the search for love with the devi at your left side. Even in this hut, your search for love cannot be dampened with wet newspapers. Are you deluding yourself into thinking your boon has been denied? In your heart you know you've received what you want.'

So saying she placed Labanya next to Amit and her right hand within his right hand. She then unclasped the gold chain from Labanya's neck and with it fastened their hands together, exclaiming, 'May your union never wane!'

---

[70] Mastuto or relating to the maternal side of the family.

Both Labanya and Amit bent to touch her feet. She said, 'Wait a bit, I'll fetch some flowers from the garden.' Yogamaya went off in the car to get some flowers. The two quietly sat side by side on the cot for a long time. Then Labanya lifted her face to Amit's and murmured, 'Why didn't you come even once the whole day?'

Amit's rueful answer was laced with laughter, 'The reason is so very trivial, it requires great courage to say it today, of all days. History doesn't record anywhere that, as a raincoat wasn't at hand, a lover postponed his visit to his beloved. Instead, it records a lover braving all the elements and swimming across wild waters. But since that is a history of the heart, why should anyone suppose that I'm not swimming there, fighting the elements? Will I ever manage to reach the shores?

For we are bound where mariner has not yet dared to go,
And we will risk the ship, ourselves and all.

Bonya, did you wait for me today?'

Labanya was not familiar with dissimulation – she replied honestly, 'Yes Mita, I heard your footsteps the whole day in the pitter-patter of the rain. It seemed to me as if you were traversing vast distances just to come to me. And finally you have entered into my life.'

Amit responded with poetic fervour, 'Bonya, in the very centre of my consciousness there was a huge, gaping, black void. It was the ugliest part of my life. Today it is full to the very brim – light sparkles on it, the whole sky casts its shadow on it, and it is now transformed into the most beautiful part of my being. My incessant chatter actually reflects its fullness, the sound of the waves lapping in my inner lake – I defy anyone to silence it.'

'Mita, what did you do the whole day?'

Amit answered, 'There you were, in the very core of my heart, totally silent. I wanted to tell you something – but there were no words! The rain fell constantly from the skies, and I kept demanding, "Give me words, words!"

> *O, what is this?*
> *Mysterious and uncapturable bliss*
> *That I have known, yet seems to be*
> *Simple as breath and easy as a smile,*
> *And older than the earth.'*

And Amit, giving Labanya his translation of these lines, told her, 'That's what I do, turn someone else's words into mine. If I could give tunes, then I would have appropriated Vidyapati's song completely,

> *Says Vidyapati, how will you survive*
> *Without Hari the interminable days and nights.*[71]

---

[71] Vidyapati was a Vaishnava poet of the sixteenth century. He wrote in Maithili.

If one doesn't get the person one cannot live without, then how does one live through the endless days and nights — where do I get the tune to match these words? I raise my eyes to pray now for words, now for tunes. And gods do descend with the words and the tunes, but in a bizarre case of mistaken identity, bestow both on someone else — perhaps on that Robi Thakur of yours.'

Labanya laughed and said, 'Even those who love Robi Thakur do not evoke his name as frequently as you do.'

Amit asked rather endearingly, 'Bonya, today I'm talking a bit too much, aren't I? A veritable verbal monsoon has descended within me. If you keep a daily weather-report, it would register immeasurable inches of lunacy everyday. If we were in Calcutta, I would have raced off to Moradabad with you, bursting tyres all the way. And if you had asked, "Why Moradabad?", I wouldn't be able to answer. When the flood breaks with its ceaseless chatter, it laughingly sweeps away time itself, like its own foam.'

Yogamaya came in at this moment with a basket of sunflowers, and instructed Labanya, 'Ma Labanya, touch his feet with these flowers.' This was nothing but a feminine attempt to give an external, ritual form to the intangible depths of the heart, a trait permeating women's very marrow.

Amit whispered in Labanya's ear at some point during this special day, 'Bonya, I want to put a ring on your finger.'

Labanya asked, 'Is it necessary, Mita?'

Amit abandoned all levity as he said, 'When you placed your hand within mine, I couldn't grasp the depths of such a generous giving. Poets have only talked about their beloved's faces. But the hand reflects so many secret messages of the heart. The hand expresses all of love's caresses, all its service, all the heart's tender and inexpressible language. My ring will hug your finger carrying just one word of mine – "I've received". Let this little phrase, murmuring in the language of gold, in the language of jewels, rest on your finger.'

Labanya assented, 'Very well.'

'I'll order it from Calcutta. Which is your favourite stone?'

Labanya said softly, 'I don't want a stone, a single pearl will be fine.'

Amit immediately approved, 'Excellent, so be it. I love pearls too.'

Chapter 11

The Theory of Union

Their marriage was fixed in the coming December-January (*Aghran*). Yogamaya would return to Calcutta to make all the arrangements.

Labanya told Amit, 'Your departure for Calcutta is long overdue. Till now you were torn in uncertainty and couldn't leave Shillong. Now take a holiday. Go back with a carefree heart. We will not meet again before our marriage.'

Amit was amused, 'Why adopt such a stern policy?'

Labanya said, 'The other day you were talking of simple joy. This is to ensure that simple bliss stays simple.'

Amit said appreciatively, 'These are deeply philosophical words. The other day I suspected you of being a poet, today I suspect you're a philosopher. To keep the simple totally simple, one has to be firm. If you want a simple rhyme, you have to use punctuation marks ruthlessly. If you're too greedy, and you hesitate to apply these punctuation marks, life turns into songless bonds, its rhyme gets lost. All right, I'll leave tomorrow, unexpectedly, bang in the middle of these halcyon days. It will seem like that abrupt end in the line from the *Meghnad Badh Kavya*[72] –

> *When he left for the abode of Death prematurely!*

Anyhow, I'll only be leaving the Shillong hills, and January isn't going to flee from the almanac. Do you know what I'm going to do in Calcutta?'

Labanya shook her head, 'What will you do?'

Amit said wickedly, 'Mashima is going to make all the arrangements for the wedding, but I'll have to make arrangements for the days that follow *after* the wedding. People forget that domesticity is an art, it has to be created anew every day. Bonya, do you remember the words with which Aja, the king in *Raghuvamsha*[73], had described Indumati?'

---

[72] Michael Madhusudan Dutta, an early nineteenth-century Bengali poet, who revolutionised Bengali poetry with his *Meghnad Badh Kabya*.

[73] Kalidasa, *Raghuvamsam*, 'Grihini sachiva sakhimithah, Priyashishya lalite kalabidhau, Karunabimukhena mrityuna harata tvaam, Bada kim na me hritam'.

Labanya immediately responded, '*Priyashishya lalite kalabidhau* (the dearest disciple in the fine arts).'

Amit said, 'These rules for the fine arts are meant for the married state. Most barbarians consider marriage as the actual union, and so the union that comes after it escapes their attention!'

Labanya was playful, 'Tell me what you've thought of the art of union. If you want me as your disciple, let the first lesson begin today.'

Nothing loath, Amit began to spin a web of words, 'Well then, listen. The poet creates rhyme by deliberately introducing the right breaks. To retain the beauty of a union, it also needs to be deliberately interrupted now and then. If you receive on demand, it becomes cheap and ultimately you get cheated. To actually meet a stiff price can bring great joy.'

Labanya quizzed Amit, 'Lets hear your calculations on the price.'

Amit returned, 'Wait, let me first describe the picture in my mind. The bank of the Ganga, the garden is on that side of Diamond Harbour. It takes about two hours to go up to Calcutta in a small steam launch.'

Labanya teased, 'So what's so urgently important in Calcutta?'

Amit assumed a grave expression, 'Well, right now there is no necessity in Calcutta, you know. I go to the Bar library to play chess, not for business. The attorneys have figured out work doesn't interest me, and hence my wavering attention. If there is a case of mutual settlement they hand me the brief, nothing beyond that. But I'll demonstrate the meaning of work after our marriage – not for the money but to understand the importance of life. The seed of the mango is neither edible, nor sweet and soft; but that hard core is the substance over which the soft flesh takes its form. Have you now understood the necessity for retaining the stony Calcutta? To relish the sweet all that much more a hard kernel is needed.'

Labanya, taking the cue quickly from Amit, said, 'I got it. Then I, too, need Calcutta. I also have to go to Calcutta – from ten to five.'

Amit said happily, 'No harm. But not to socialise, to work.'

Labanya said, considering the point, 'Suggest some kind of work. Without a salary?'

Amit pretended to be horrified, 'No, no, work without a salary is seventy five percent dodging! It's neither proper work, nor a holiday. If you want, you can easily become a professor in a girls' college.'

Labanya immediately said, 'Fine, I will certainly want it. Then?'

Amit was dreamy, 'I vividly see the Ganga. An ancient banyan tree with massive prop-roots rises from its nether slopes. When Dhanapati[74] was sailing to Sinhala on the Ganga, he must

---

[74]Dhanapati is one of the central characters in *the Chandi Mangalkavyas*, a range of vernacular texts written in the sixteenth and seventeenth centuries, and even later, in Bengal. Dhanapati was a rich merchant

have moored under this banyan tree and cooked here. The moss-covered ghat, with worn and cracked stone steps leading down to the river, lies to its southern side. Our slender, green and white boat is tied at the bottom, with its name written in white on its blue banner. Do give it a name.'

'Shall I?' Labanya asked eagerly. 'Mitali?'

Amit was delighted, 'Perfect name – Mitali. I had thought of "Sagari", and was feeling quite smug about it, but I own defeat. A thin rivulet runs through the garden, pulsing to the beat of the Ganga. On that side is your house, on this side, mine.'

Labanya dreamily added, 'Will you be swimming across every day? I'll put out a light at a window for you.'

Amit was suddenly practical, 'I'll swim metaphorically, on the narrow wooden bridge stretching across. Your house is called "Manasi". Give my house a name.'

Labanya softly said, '"Deepak".'

Pleased, Amit said, 'Just the right name. To suit its name a lamp will burn on the roof of my house, a red light for the evenings when we meet and a blue light for the evenings we don't. I'll expect an invitation letter from you everyday upon my return from Calcutta. There should be an element of

---

and a devotee of Shiva. How he and his family also became devotees of Chandi, Shiva's consort, is the core theme of the *Chandi Mangalkavyas*. There are various kinds of *Mangalkavyas*, centering on Manasa, and other minor gods and goddesses, all trying to legitimise the new entrant into the established pantheon of gods and goddesses.

uncertainty here – maybe I'll get the invitation, maybe not. If I don't get the invitation by eight in the evening, I'll curse my luck and try to read Bertrand Russell's *Logic*. Our rules shall totally ban my visits to your house without an invitation.'

Labanya asked quickly, 'What about my visits to your house?'

'The same rule should apply to both, but it wouldn't be unbearable if there are some occasional lapses,' Amit, gravely conceded, giving the matter due consideration.

'If the occasional lapses have no chance of becoming a rule, I think I shall visit your house in a burqua! It will be such a mess!' said Labanya, her housewifely instincts surfacing.

Amit was not diverted. 'Do that. But I want my invitation letter. It needn't contain more than a couple of lines from some poem.'

Labanya re-entered the dream and demanded, 'What about my invitation letter? Am I to be ostracised?'

Amit instantly said, 'Once every month, when the fifteenth day assumes glorious wholeness against the fragmented beauty of the previous fourteen days on the full-moon night, you will get your letter.'

Labanya demanded, 'Let's hear a sample of a letter to your dear disciple.'

'All right.' Amit promptly whipped out a notebook from his pocket, tore off a page, and scribbled,

Blow gently over my garden
Wind of the southern sea

> *In the hour my love cometh*
> *And calleth me.*

Labanya did not return the piece of paper.

Amit demanded in his turn, 'Now you give me a sample, let's see if your education has progressed.'

Labanya was about to write on a piece of paper, but Amit handed her his notebook, 'Write it here,' he said.

Labanya wrote —

> *Mita, thou art my life, thou art my ornament,*
> *Thou art the very pearl from my life's ocean.*

Amit pocketed the notebook and said, 'Strangely, my lines reflect a feminine cast of mind, yours a masculine cast, but it is not inappropriate. And why should they be? Even if the wood comes from different trees, the fire blazing from both assumes the same form.'

Labanya asked, 'The invitations have been sent out, what now?'

Amit became lyrical, 'The evening star is in the sky, Ganga is at high tide, the wind has begun to rustle through the rows of conifer trees, the water is lapping at the roots of the old banyan tree. There is a lotus lake behind your house, you've just had your evening bath there, in the quiet privacy of your backyard, and have finished tying your hair! As your sarees change colour every day, I will be wondering about this evening's colour as I walk towards your house. Our meeting places are also never fixed – sometimes it is under the paved area under the champak tree, then maybe on the terrace, then again it might be near the Ganga. I, too, would have bathed in the Ganga, and would have donned a white fine dhoti and chaddar, and on my feet will be a pair of khadam[75] inlaid with ivory. When I reach the spot, you'll be sitting on a rich carpet, with a heavy garland on a silver platter, sandalpaste in a bowl and incense sticks burning in the corner. During the pujas, the two of us will travel for at least two months. But the places will be different – if you go to the mountains then I head towards the seaside. I have now presented my booklet on domestic rules – what do you say?'

'I don't mind it,' Labanya replied quietly.

Amit said a little anxiously, 'Bonya, there is a lot of difference between "not minding" and "appealing to the mind"!'

Labanya said, 'I still would not object if what is necessary to you is unnecessary for me.'

Amit was shocked, 'It's not necessary for you!'

There was a sad note in Labanya' voice. 'No, none. Even if you stay very close to me, there is still a great deal of distance between us. It's therefore superfluous to make up rules to induce a certain distance. I'm very aware I've got nothing that can unflinchingly, unashamedly bear your gaze from very close quarters. It's certainly safe for me to have our houses on either side of the rivulet.'

---

[75] Khadam are a form of indigenous footwear, normally made of wood. It is like a plank, and the big toe and middle toe grip a small knob.

Amit sprang from the couch and burst out emotionally, impetuously, 'To hell with my garden, I won't let you worst me! I won't move a foot out of Calcutta. I will hire a room for seventy-five rupees a month, immediately above Niranjan's office! You and I will stay there. In the geography of the mind, distance is not judged in real terms. On the three and a half foot bed, your Mahal Manasi on the left, and my Mahal Deepak on the right, will fit in very snugly. Against the east-facing wall, we'll have a mirrored wardrobe – you and I can see our faces there! The western wall will house the bookshelf – with its back it'll ward off the sun, and its front will contain the one and only circulating library for these two readers. The northern section of the room will have a sofa, where I'll sit, leaving a little space on the left. You'll stand behind the alna.[76] Two feet away, from the sofa, I'll hold up in my trembling hand my invitation letter. On it will be written,

> *Blow gently, gently, over the terrace*
> *O thou southern wind*
> *At the moment my beloved's eyes*
> *Mine own do gently meet.*

Is this sounding bad, Bonya?'

Labanya was reassuring, 'Quite the contrary, Mita. Where did you get it from?'

---

[76]Alnā – clotheshorse

Amit said smugly, 'From my friend, Neel Madhav's notebook. He wasn't exactly sure of the timing of his would-be-bride's arrival in his life. In anticipation he had remoulded this English poem in the Calcutta style, as an ode to this lady, and I helped him with it somewhat. After completing MA in Economics, he brought home his bride, who was dowered with fifteen thousand rupees in cash, and eighty bhoris of gold ornaments. Four eyes have met, the southern breeze also blows, but the poem lies unused. Now its other owner shouldn't feel hesitant in claiming the entire poem for his own use.'

Labanya needled Amit a bit, 'The southern breeze will presumably blow over your terrace as well, but will your new bride always remain new?'

Amit immediately smashed his fist on the table, yelling, 'Always, always, always!!'

Yogamaya hurriedly entered from the next room and asked, 'What will stay for always? It seems my poor table is not destined to be here for always.'

Amit declared, 'Whatever is durable will endure in this world. New brides are rare in human society, but if by some extraordinary chance, there is one such, she will remain the new bride forever.'

Labanya demanded, 'Show me a single instance.'

Amit, equally adamantly, replied, 'I'll show you one when the time comes.'

Yogamaya said to appease them, 'I think you'll have to wait a while for that. In the meanwhile, come and eat.'

Chapter 12

The Last Evening

After the meal, Amit announced, 'I'm leaving for Calcutta tomorrow, Mashima. My relatives have a strong suspicion that I have suddenly turned Khasia'.

Yogamaya inquired, 'Are your relatives aware of such a possibility being possible?'

'Of course they know,' Amit affirmed, 'otherwise they wouldn't be relatives! But that doesn't mean I change at a word, or into a Khasia. This is not just a change of caste! This is a millennial change! With a kalpa[77] in between. The Creator has

---

[77] A mythical measurement of cyclical time: one Divyayuga, comprising of the Satya, Treta, Dwapar, and Kali, approximately is equivalent to 43 lakhs 20 thousand years, and roughly 71 such Divyayuga comprise

himself awoken within me! Do consent to the two of us going for a walk, Mashima! I want us to pay our joint salutation to these Shillong hills before I leave.'

Yogamaya consented. As they went off, they drew close to each other, while their fingers entwined involuntarily. Alongside the deserted road, the deep forests arose and sloped away, down, far down. There was a gap in this denseness: just here, the sky had been left unguarded by the watchful mountain range, and it had scooped up the last of the red, westering sunlight. The two finally halted and stood facing the west. Amit drew Labanya to his breast, and tilted her face to his. Tears were trickling from the corners of Labanya's half-closed eyes. The ruby and emerald hues cast over the last golden glow of the sun began fading. A beautiful, deep and pure azure gleamed occasionally through the thin clouds, hinting at the unutterable, disembodied, celestial bliss ineffably permeating the heavens. Gradually, the darkness thickened. The little patch of open sky, like the flowers at night, tightly furled its many-coloured petals.

From the shelter of Amit's breast, Labanya whispered, 'Let's go back now.' She intuitively felt that this was the perfect moment to end their walk. Amit's heart also echoed Labanya's intuition. He wordlessly pressed Labanya's face against his breast one final time before turning very slowly homewards.

---

one day in Brahma's time-scale. Many such days amount to one Brahmakalpa. Therefore 'kalpa' conveys a sense of limitless time. However, there are many opinions in this calculation.

Presently he said, 'I won't visit you again before I leave tomorrow morning.'

'Why won't you?' Labanya asked.

Amit's words echoed her innermost thoughts, 'Today, our Shillong phase has halted at exactly the right moment – the end of the first canto – our own Prelude to paradise.'

Labanya walked silently at Amit's side, her hand in his. Dammed-up tears were mingled with an intense joy in her heart. She was haunted by a strange foreboding that never again would she be so intimately close to the unimaginable. The bridal chamber seemed strangely removed from their deep exchange of glances at this divine moment. This moment was real, heady with their union, heavy with the pain of separation, and it seemed fitting to Labanya that she should bow before Amit, touch his feet, and render up her sense of fulfilment to Amit in the emotionally charged words – 'You have indeed bestowed on me great blessedness.' But the words remained unsaid, locked within her full heart.

As they neared the house, Amit requested, 'Bonya, give me your last few words in verse – something my mind can bear away with ease – any little thing you remember.'

After a little thought, Labanya softly recited,

'No happiness have I given you, only left freedom's offering,
As the light dispelled the night. I've ended all, leaving nothing
Of pleading prayers, of the poverty of wasted moments piling,

Of false pride, of weak tears, the proud smiles of leave-taking,
No backward glances. Merely the gift of freedom I'm capable of giving
I give today, by rendering up my own noble death in this offering.'

The verse shook Amit. He said passionately, 'This is wrong, very wrong, Bonya! Such words at such a moment shouldn't have come! Why did they occur to you? Take them back!'

Labanya said sweetly, reassuringly, 'Why be afraid, Mita? This is love that has been sacralised by the sacrificial fire, it does not make its own demands for happiness. Because it is free, it can bestow freedom. It does not bring tiredness, or dullness in its wake — it is the supreme gift of love.'

Amit however, insisted, 'But I want to know where you got this poem from?'

'It is Robi Thakur's,' came the reply.

Amit was very surprised, 'But I haven't seen it in any of his books.'

'It hasn't been published.'

Amit's curiosity was piqued. 'Then how did you get it?'

Labanya answered, 'There was a young boy who held my father to be his guru. My father would give him food for the mind, but his heart also yearned for food. He would go to Robi Thakur whenever he could spare some time and beg for some verses.'

Amit comprehended instantly. 'And he would offer them up at your feet.'

Labanya said, 'He did not have such temerity. Hoping they would attract my notice, that I might pick them up, he would leave them lying about.'

'Were you kind to him?' Amit asked.

Labanya said simply, 'I did not get the chance. But I pray from the bottom of my heart that God will be kind to him.'

Amit remarked thoughtfully, 'I think the poem you recited actually spoke the language of that unfortunate's heart.'

Labanya said with simple honesty, 'Yes, it is his heart's language.'

'Then why did it come to your mind today?' Amit asked forcefully.

Labanya said gravely, 'How can I tell? But along with these lines a few more lines have come to my mind. Why I can't tell –

O Beautiful, you bring to eyes only tears,
To the heart you have brought sorrow that sears.
In that crucible of pain burning sharp,
Is banished spells binding the heart.
In its heated breath, when exhaled,
There bloom the lotuses of separation by the hundreds.'

Amit gripped Labanya's hand violently and asked, 'Labanya, why has that boy come between us? This isn't my jealousy speaking, I hold jealousy in contempt. But an unknown fear has really touched my heart. Tell me why you recalled the poems he had presented, in this, of all moments.'

Labanya replied, 'After he bade farewell and left our house, I found these two poems inside the desk he used to write at. There were also some other unpublished poems of Robi Thakur, almost filling an entire notebook. Today I'm taking leave of you, and possibly that's why the poems flashed into my mind.'

Amit, still slightly distressed, said, 'Is there no difference between this leave-taking and that leave-taking?'

With a quiet gravity, Labanya replied, 'I can't answer that. But this argument is not necessary. I have merely recited what appealed to me. There need be no other reason.'

Amit declared, 'Bonya, until the day Robi Thakur's poetry is not forgotten, the reality of his writing will not reveal itself. For this reason I don't even use his poems. The approval of a coterie is like the damp hand of a fog darkening the light of the sky.'

Labanya said firmly, 'Look Mita, women reserve their personal preferences for their exclusive use within the antahpur.[78] They don't keep tabs on fashionable opinions. For that they pay whatever they can give, without bothering to compare market rates.'

Amit said on a lighter note, 'Oh, then I also have hope, Bonya! I'll hide my actual market rate, and proudly display the high price-tag you label me with.'

---

[78] Antahpur or the interior of the house where the women resided.

Labanya also replied in a lighter vein, 'We are very close to the house, Mita – let me hear your poem marking the journey's end.'

Slipping back in his teasing mood, Amit said, 'Don't be annoyed, Bonya, I can't mouth Robi Thakur's poems.'

Labanya said seriously, 'Why should I get annoyed, Mita?'

Amit, in his incorrigible manner, said, 'I have discovered a poet, his style...'

Labanya broke in, 'I often hear you mention him. I've written to some publishers in Calcutta to send me some of his works.'

Amit exclaimed in horrified accents, 'Goodness! His works! The fellow has many faults, but approaching the publishers with manuscripts isn't one of them. You will get to know about him through me, and only me! Otherwise...'

Labanya interrupted again, 'Don't worry, Mita, I'm confident I shall be able to grasp his works the way you grasp his writings. I'll still win.'

Amit demanded, 'How?'

Labanya was a little teasing, 'What I get through my own likes, will stay mine, and what I get through your likes will also become mine. My measure for absorption will include both our tastes. I'll still be able to fit both the poets on that bookshelf in that little room you were speaking of. So recite your poem.'

Amit said moodily, 'I don't feel like reciting it now. So much argument has ruined the environment.'

Labanya said soothingly, 'The environment is fine. Say it.'

Amit then pushed his hair up and away from his face, and recited with great emotion –

> *'Beautiful one, O you morning star*
> *Sparkling across the mountain peaks afar,*
> *When the tired night is on the wane*
> *Shine with hope on the lost wayfarer.'*

Amit then deluged Labanya with his comments, 'You see Bonya, the moon has called out to the morning star as it longs for company in the still watches of the night. It is weary of its own nights –

> *Where the earth the sky does meet*
> *I, the moon, just half-awake, do shine,*
> *On the breast of darkness*
> *A thin crescent of listless light.*

Its weak light has barely scratched the dense darkness. This is its regret. Its very feebleness has become a net, and even while asleep at night, it struggles to free itself from itself in little spurts. What an idea! Grand!

> *My place is reserved*
> *In the deeply asleep universe*
> *I play out a tune in my dreams*
> *Shaking slightly out of my slumbers.*

But to live without any weight creates weariness, like a tired, apathetic river, unable to bear the burden of its stagnant water and sediment. So the moon says in self-pity,

> *Yet travelling with dragging steps*
> *My journey draws to a close,*
> *My melody keeps dying mid-way*
> *Tiredness strangles the final notes.*

But this tiredness is not the end. Again the moon is hopeful of re-tuning the loose strings of his veena, as footsteps approaching him from across the universe promise him succour –

> *Beautiful one, O you morning star,*
> *Hasten here ere the night departs*
> *When in dreams the words all scatter,*
> *As the morning breaks gather them together.*

There was yet the hope of a rescue, the great hubbub of the universe was striking his ears, and the messenger from that great Pathway was coming, lamp in hand –

> *Raise it from the abyss of darkness*
> *Take it for the morning bright*
> *It had forgotten itself in the blackness*
> *Let it be thankful in the light.*
> *Where slumber itself evaporates,*

THE LAST EVENING

> *Whence comes that universal great chant*
> *There I offer up my music*
> *I, the moon, hanging in the sky at night.'*

And Amit informed Labanya, 'I am that wretched moon. I'm leaving tomorrow morning. But I don't want to leave that space empty – and so I call upon the arrival of the beautiful morning star, to hail the presage of the dawn. Whatever was hazy in the dreamy darkness, will be restored to wholeness and clarity at daybreak by the beautiful morning star. The poem has optimism, it grandly celebrates the coming morning. Your Robi Thakur will never come near it with his pessimistic mourning.'

Labanya was full of gentle remonstrance, 'Why are you getting angry, Mita? Is there any use harping on Robi Thakur's limitations?'

'You all make such a lot of fuss about him ...,' Amit grumbled.

'Don't say that, Mita. My liking is my very own, and if it does not agree with yours or anyone else's, it's not my fault. If you like, we can have an agreement – if I ever get a place in that seventy-five rupee, rented room of yours, then you can quote your poet, but I won't from mine.' Labanya was all sweet reasonableness.

Amit protested, 'But that's not fair. Marriage is all about mutual submission to tyranny – it shouldn't be one sided.'

Labanya said wisely, 'You won't be able to stand the torment of a different taste. At the feast of taste, you don't allow anyone entry without invitation, but I welcome all guests.'

Amit said penitently, 'I shouldn't have begun this argument. The melody of our last evening together has been spoiled.'

Labanya said, 'Certainly not! The melody, which rings true even after all has been said, is our melody. It has a bottomless capacity to forgive.'

Amit was determined to make amends, 'I have to rid my mouth of its bad taste. But it can't be done with Bengali poetry. I tend to be far more balanced when it comes to English poetry. After I had returned from England, I had even taught for a while.'

Labanya laughed and said in self-mockery, 'Our sense of judgment is like an English bulldog's – as soon as he sees the dhoti's pleats twitching, he barks! He can't quite tell what *is* respectable in that sartorial range! Yet his tail wags at a bearer's uniform!'

Amit replied in kind, 'I must agree! It's not normal to be biased. It's made to order in most cases. Our very training coerces us to be biased about English literature. We dare not criticise one kind of literature because of that training, or go against the established opinion and call another brand good. Anyway, even Nibaran Chakraborty is banned today, it'll be untranslated English poetry.'

Labanya protested, 'No, no, Mita, nothing English. That can be done at the table at home! It has to be Nibaran Chakraborty this last evening, nobody else will do!'

Delighted, Amit exclaimed, 'Glory to Nibaran Chakraborty! He has achieved immortality! Bonya, I'll turn him into your court poet. Only at your door will he accept laurels!'

'Will he always be satisfied with that?' Labanya inquired.
Amit said, 'If he isn't I'll chuck him out by his ear!'
'I'll think about his punishment later; now recite it!
Amit declaimed,

> 'With such patience night and day
> Next to me you stayed.
> The imprints of your footsteps
> Often did fall on the dusty path of my destiny.
> Today as I depart for a distant destination,
> I offer you my gift, a song singing your glory.
>
> Life's futile arrangements incomplete
> have kept the sacrificial fires unlit.
> Spiralling smoke drifted away on a hopeless sigh
> In the empty sky.
> Often a weak, momentary flare
>   Has ineffectually marked
>   the inert forehead of the night,
> and vanished, without a trace, into the void of time.
>   Now at your advent
>   the sacred fire has kindled
>   into a proud, crackling blaze.
> My yajna[79] is indeed blessed.
> My homage at the end of the day

---

79. Yajna or a ritualistic sacrificial ceremony.

I offer up in your name.
Over your acceptance of my salutations
Is life's fulfilment pronounced.
On this obeisance of mine
Place your fond hand in a gentle touch.
If you beckon me before your glory,
Where enthroned you preside,
There let my homage reside.'

Chapter 13

Apprehension

It was difficult for Labanya to concentrate on her work the next morning. She hadn't even gone for her usual walk. Amit had declared that he didn't wish to meet on the morning he was leaving Shillong. Both were determined to protect the vow. So Labanya, aware that her usual route would lead her through the very path Amit would have to take, hadn't ventured on her daily constitutional. The eagerness in her heart had to be reined in tightly. Yogamaya normally got up very early, bathed, and then picked some flowers for her morning prayers. Even before Yogamaya had entered the garden, Labanya had crossed it and headed for the eucalyptus trees. She had a couple of books in her hand — perhaps to mislead others as well as herself. The book lay open, the morning got on, but the pages remained unturned. One thought kept recurring in her heart – the great celebration in her life had come to an end. It seemed as though the transient clouds scudding across the morning sky were being swept away by some harbinger of disaster. She was convinced that once he had moved away, Amit's escapist nature would allow him to forget this interlude easily. It was like beginning a story while walking companionably with a traveller on the road: then night arrives. The new day reveals that the thread of the story had snapped, and the traveller was long gone. Labanya was dismally pondering over her own tale that would now never have an ending. The dreariness of this incomplete story seemed to have touched the morning light. The premature ending of the story, with its accompanying listlessness, was reflected in the moist wind.

When it was about nine in the morning, suddenly Amit rushed in, loudly calling out, 'Mashima, Mashima!' Yogamaya had finished her early-morning meditation, and was making arrangements for the day's domestic needs in the pantry. Her heart, too, was very heavy today. Her days and her affections had been increasingly filled with Amit's laughter, words and waywardness. The painful knowledge of his departure had made her morning move leadenly, like a bloom weighed down by a dew-drop. She had not called Labanya to help her in her domestic tasks, dragging painfully along today. She had understood Labanya's need to be alone, out of the range of curious glances.

Labanya shot to her feet. The book dropped from her lap, but she didn't even register it. Yogamaya too, hurried out from the pantry, and asked, 'What is it Amit? An earthquake?'

'Very much an earthquake!' came the response. 'I had sent off my luggage, the car was ready. I had just popped down to the post office to check my mail and I found a telegram there!'

His agitated face made Yogamaya ask anxiously, 'Is everything all right at home?'

Labanya also came into the room at this point. Amit, with distress writ large on his face, announced, 'Sissy, my sister, her friend, Katy Mittir[80], and Katy's elder brother, Noren, are all arriving here this very evening!'

Yogamaya said soothingly, 'So what's the problem, Baba. There is an unoccupied house next to the race-course – so I've heard. If that's unavailable, there's enough space here for everyone.'

With no abatement of his anxiety, Amit said, 'That doesn't worry me at all! They have telegrammed to book hotel rooms for themselves.'

Yogamaya was still in the dark, but changed the subject, 'Anyway, I won't allow your sisters to find out you're staying in that poky, graceless, hole of a house. They will lay the blame for the lunacy of their own family member on our heads.'

Amit shook his head, 'No, Mashi, my paradise is lost! I'm banished from that furnitureless, naked, heaven. The dreams will all fly away from the haven of that ropy cot! I shall have to relocate to a fastidiously clean, highly civilised, hotel room!'

---

[80]Mittir or the Bengali colloquial form of Mitra. The anglicised version is Mitter.

Amit's words were certainly not alarming, but Labanya turned pale. It had not even occurred to her till now that Amit's social circle was very far removed from her own. But in a sudden flash she comprehended this. There had been no harsh picture of separation in Amit's planned departure for Calcutta. But this social compulsion on Amit to shift to a hotel revealed to her the sheer improbability of their dreams of a life together in a home they had already built with their imaginations.

Amit glanced briefly at Labanya and then remarked to Yogamaya, 'Whether I go to a hotel or to hell, this will always be my real home.'

Amit had a feeling in his bones that Calcutta was bringing nothing good. His mind was busily engaged in turning over various plans which would prevent Sissy's crowd from coming to Yogamaya's house. Unfortunately, all his mail had been redirected to Yogamaya's house for quite some time, as he had no inkling of anything dangerous coming of it. Amit could not keep his anxieties to himself; on the contrary, he exaggerated his feelings. Even Yogamaya couldn't help feeling that his distress at the prospect of his sisters' imminent arrival was certainly excessive. As for Labanya, she immediately concluded that Amit was ashamed of her before his sisters. For Labanya the whole matter became sordid and humiliating.

Amit asked Labanya, 'Do you have time? Would you like to come for a walk?'

Labanya's voice was frosty, 'No, there's no time.'

Yogamaya said quickly, 'Go, dear, go for a walk.'

'Kartama, I've really not paid much attention to Surama's education over the last few weeks. It's been very wrong of me. I had resolved last night that from today there would be no laxity.' And Labanya pressed her lips firmly together.

That good lady knew Labanya in this mood and did not dare attempt further persuasion.

Amit said dryly, 'I may as well do my duty then, I'm off to make all the arrangements for them.'

As Amit prepared to leave, he suddenly stood still, stared into the distance, and said, 'Bonya, look there! You can see the roof of my house almost hidden by the trees. I haven't told you something, I've bought that house. The owner was pretty surprised. She must have thought I had discovered a gold-mine there. She certainly hiked up her price. I had discovered a gold-mine all right, but only I know its location. My tumble-down hut's hidden wealth will be hidden from all eyes.'

A dark shadow passed over Labanya's face. She said, 'Why do you always think of other people? What if they do come to know? It is necessary for them to know of certain things for only then they won't dare to be rude.'

Amit evaded this and instead declared, 'Bonya, I've made up my mind to stay in that house for a while after we get married. The garden on the banks of the Ganga, the ghat, the banyan tree – that house has absorbed it all. It indeed lives up to the name you gave it – Mitali.'

Labanya said gently, 'You've emerged from that house today, Mita. If ever you feel like returning there, you'll find it's shrunk.

The haven of today may not offer the same space tomorrow. The other day you said the first sadhana of human beings is for poverty, and then for glorious wealth. You did not speak of the last — it is that of tyaaga, of letting go.'

Amit was impatient, 'Bonya, that's your Robi Thakur talking. He says, today Shah Jahan has even outdistanced the Taj Mahal. Your poet's imagination boggles at the thought that we create something just so that we can step beyond it. This is called evolution in human civilisation. A demon of chaos possesses you and says compellingly, "Create!" As soon as you create, it is exorcised, but the creation itself becomes an unnecessary adjunct of the act of creation. But this letting go of the beautiful things we create is not the last, final word. The world always has and always will create a stream of Shah Jahans and Mumtazes. They were not the only pair of lovers in the world. That's why the Taj Mahal could never free itself of the human presence. Nibaran Chakraborty has written a poem on the nuptial chamber — a kind of short answer to your poet's writing on the Taj Mahal — and its written on a postcard —

You'll soon be bereft,
The night turns restless
At the morning's public hum,
And turns away her mysteriously shadowed face.
Alas, nuptial chamber, guardian of sacred human union!
The boundless space without,
The robber of bliss,

> *Stands just outside your door,*
> *And pronounces the sentence of separation.*
> *As the outside breaks in,*
> *The garlands exchanged by loving hands, lie torn,*
> *The flowers are scattered, your reign is over.*
> *Yet not so! Changeless, you'll always exist,*
> *Every day.*
> *Your celebration never ends,*
> *Your voice is never silent,*
> *The twain has never left you,*
> *Your conjugal bed is never empty,*
> *They have never left at all.*
> *They keep coming back in ever-fresh pairs,*
> *At your beckoning,*
> *And stand before your generous door.*
> *O you nuptial chamber,*
> *You will always exist, because in the universe love is immortal.*

Robi Thakur keeps talking of leave-taking, but he doesn't know how to sing the song of abiding. Bonya, does the poet mean to say that the door won't swing open at our knock?'

Labanya responded to this quite sharply, 'Mita, keep a request, will you? Don't bring up the subject of our ever-duelling poets this morning. Do you think I haven't known from the very first day that Nibaran Chakraborty is none other than you? Don't start building a memorial for our love in that poem of yours. At least wait for it to die first!'

Labanya was aware of some deep inner agitation within Amit which compelled him to talk ceaselessly as a cover. Amit too, realised the inappropriateness of their poetical debates this morning, which had been perfectly apt the evening before. But he did not relish the ease with which Labanya had understood this. He said dryly, 'I suppose I must go, I too have work in the world, and right now it means a survey of the hotel. It seems that poor Nibaran Chakraborty's race is run.'

Labanya was suddenly pleading, 'Look Mita, I hope you can always find it within you to forgive me. If one day, the time to depart does arrive, I beg of you, don't go away with anger in your heart.' Labanya then hurried away to hide her welling tears.

Amit stood still for a while. Then absentmindedly he ambled towards the eucalyptus trees. He noticed a few walnut shells scattered there, and there was a strange pang in his heart. It seemed to him that as life moved on, the debris it left in its wake was indeed pathetic in its very triviality. Robi Thakur's *Balaka* lying on the grass, caught his attention next. Its bottom-most leaf was damp. At first he thought of returning it, but he pocketed it instead. Then he toyed with the idea of going off to the hotel, but he didn't do that either; just folded up on the grass under the trees. The wet clouds of last night had sponged the sky squeaky clean. The picturesque scenery stretching away in all directions stood out clearly in the freshly-washed breeze. The outlines of the mountains and the trees were sharply etched against the deep blue of the sky. It almost seemed as if the world had advanced till it touched the mind. The morning was rolling by, humming to itself the Bhairabi raga.

Labanya was wholly determined to get down to her tasks immediately. But when from a distance she saw Amit sitting under the trees, her resolution broke, her heart felt suffocated, and her eyes pooled. She drew close and asked, 'What are you thinking about, Mita?'

Amit replied, 'The very opposite of my thoughts over all these days.'

Labanya was a little resigned, 'You don't keep well if you don't get to see your own mind upside down now and then. So tell me, what are these thoughts in reverse-gear?'

Amit said slowly, 'I've been mentally building a home with you in my heart – sometimes next to the Ganga, sometimes on a mountain. Today I see in my mind's eye a road for our journey, bathed in a pensive morning light – through the shady forests and over the mountains. A long staff with an iron point is in my hand, on my back a square haversack with leather straps. You'll be with me. You certainly live up to your name, for you have swept me out of the enclosing four walls and cut me loose. There are so many people inside the house, but the road is just for the two of us.'

Labanya was really amused, 'The garden in Diamond Harbour has long gone, and now the poor room, cheap at seventy-five rupees, has joined it! Well, let it! But how are we to maintain our distance – at the end of each day's journey do we head for different rest-houses?'

Amit said, 'That won't be necessary. Movement itself keeps us young, at every step there is newness, and no time to get old. Age creeps up when we sit still.'

Labanya asked curiously, 'Why have you suddenly got this idea in your head?'

Amit said, 'Then listen. I've received a letter from Shobhanlal unexpectedly – you must have heard of him – the fellow who got the Premchand-Roychand scholarship. He wanted to find out about the old historical routes criss-crossing the length and breadth of India and so he has hit the road. He wants to rediscover the lost roads of the past. I wish to create the road to the future.'

Something very heavy struck Labanya's heart a massive blow. She cut Amit short and asked quickly, 'I appeared for my MA exams in the same year as Shobhanlal. I would like to hear a little bit more of him.'

Amit said ruminatively, 'At one time he was mad to unearth an old route running through the ancient town of Kapish in Afghanistan. This was the route Hieun Tsang had taken to come to India. Long before that, Alexander had taken the same route on his military campaign. He learnt Pushtu pretty well and mastered many mannerisms of the Pathans. His delicately beautiful frame in those loose garments looked more Persian than Pathan. He approached me with a request: as the French scholars were working in this area, could I provide him with a letter of reference? When I was in France some of them had taught me. I gave a letter, but he didn't get permission from the

Government of India. From then onwards, he has been seeking these old routes high and low through the rugged Himalayas, sometimes in Kashmir, sometimes in Kumaon. This time he desires to extend his search to the eastern Himalayas as well. He now wants to find out the different paths Buddhism took, to spread to various parts of the world. I too become pensive when I remember that road-lunatic. We look into texts to trace out roads, and damage our eyes – that madcap is out looking for the text of the road, written by the hand of human civilisation itself. Do you know what I think?'

Labanya said, 'No, do tell.'

Amit said, 'In the first flush of youth, Shobhanlal must have been roughly pushed aside by a delicate hand – its force tumbled him out of the home into the road. I don't know his history well, but one day he and I were chatting away – time slipped away in conversation and we suddenly realised it was the middle of the night. The moon had ridden up in the sky and was then behind a flowering tree, and he almost mentioned somebody. He did not name her, gave no description, but his voice thickened with emotion even as he entered the fringes of his memory, and he hurriedly left. I realised that there was an intensely cruel memory tormenting him. Maybe it is this memory he wants to expunge by walking endlessly on the road.'

Labanya suddenly developed a keen interest in botany, and bent over to study a little yellow-and-white wild flower. It became necessary to count its individual petals with scientific concentration.

Amit said conversationally, 'You know Bonya, today you've pushed me out into the road.'

Labanya asked, 'How did I do that?'

Amit said a little wistfully, 'I had built a home. When I heard you speak this morning, it seemed to me you were reluctant to step into it. For two months now, I had mentally arranged and rearranged it. I then invited you – I said, "Come love, step into this home." But you took off your bridal attire, and said, "Friend, this place is too constricting – we will take the seven steps together for the rest of our lives."'

Further display of interest in botany was impossible. Labanya sprang to her feet, and barely managed to say in a faltering voice, 'No more Mita, there isn't any time.'

Chapter 14
Dhumketu or Haley's Comet

A fact had just swum into Amit's line of vision – the entire Bengali community in Shillong knew of his relationship with Labanya. The clerical staff in government offices gave top priority to hot gossip on the appearance of new planetary kings and ministers in their secretarial-skies. But the sudden appearance of a stellar pair in the human solar system with a luminosity of the first magnitude threw them off track. Discussions issued volubly from all the acute observers of this engrossing human drama, with these two newly shining stars as the cast.

Kumar Mukhujje[81], an attorney – was sucked into this verbal vortex when he went up to savour the fresh air in the hills. His name had been satirically abridged to Kumar Mukho[82] by some and to Mar Mukho by others, certainly not without reason. Though not an intimate inmate of the inner circle of Sissy's friends, he could touch its fringes as an acquaintance. Amit had nicknamed him *Dhumketu*[83] *Mukho* after the Haley's Comet,[83] for he was capable of sweeping his tail over their social group without being a part of it. Everybody wickedly guessed that the planet exerting its magnetic pull over *Mukho* was Lissy, but Lissy herself was both embarrassed and angry at the joke. So she frequently and viciously stamped on his tail. But as far as I could see, with no effect on either his head or his tail – they remained intact.

Amit has glimpsed Kumar *Mukho* on the streets of Shillong every now and then. It is quite difficult not to. Though he hasn't so far set foot in England, his English mannerisms are flashily evident. A fat cheroot is a constant presence between his teeth, which has earned him his nickname – *Dhumketu Mukho*. Amit has tried to avoid him by giving him a wide berth, and has fondly hoped that he has managed to evade *Dhumketu's* eyes. But to notice without seeming to is an art – like the art of stealing

---

[81] Mukhujje or the colloquial form of Mukhopadhyay. The anglicised version is Mukerji/Mukherjee.

[82] *Mukho* is a peculiarly Bengali term for a facial form. Maar *Mukho* or person who looks like he is aggressive.

[83] Haley's Comet

which is fine until one is caught. One has to really master the skill of looking beyond the person in front of you.

From the Bengali community in Shillong, Kumar Mukho had now collected a voluminous body of stories which might be broadly summed up under the title, 'The Story of Amit Rai'. Those who were the most abusive were secretly the most amused. Kumar had arrived in Shillong determined to stay for some time and get his digestive tracts in good working order. However, the raw excitement of having a tale to tell drove him back to Calcutta within five days. Once there, his wild exaggerations, blown out with his cheroot smoke, created panic not unmixed with merriment and curiosity in the Sissy-Lissy circle.

The experienced reader would have fathomed by now that Noren, Katy Mitter's elder brother, was the Goddess Sissy's vehicle. Noren had been a devoted vehicle, hoping that the firm nuptial knot would be his reward. Sissy's heart was willing but she coyly refused to forego her feminine mystique with an open avowal of her acceptance. Noren just couldn't be sure of her. Still, he was hopeful of the final outcome with Amit's consent and counsel. But as that humbug refused to return to Calcutta, or even answer his urgent letters, Noren hurled the choicest English invectives at the absent Amit publicly and privately. He even telegraphed his displeasure most graphically to Shillong – but like ineffectual rockets aimed at a distant star, these vanished without a trace. Still, everyone unanimously agreed about the necessity for an on-the-spot assessment of the situation. Amit was being borne away on a strong, disastrous current and it behoved his friends to grab him by any part of his anatomy — even if it be a tuft of hair — and safely haul him to shore. Katy, someone else's sister, was far more enthusiastic in this matter than Sissy, Amit's own sister. Katy Mitter's concern strikingly resembled that of our politicians bemoaning the disappearance of India's wealth into foreign coffers.

Noren Mitter had lived long in Europe. The son of a rich zamindar, he was untroubled with money or about squandering it. His concern for *attaining* an education was similarly light. He had concentrated on *spending* — both money and time — while in Europe. He had desired a quick promotion to an irresponsible independence and unmerited self-respect — and so had hankered after an artist's life. Doggedly trailing the tracks of the Goddess Saraswati, patroness of the fine arts, he had lived in the Bohemian quarters of many European cities. But as blunt well-wishers rudely requested him to abandon his pretensions as a painter, he stopped wielding the paint-brush. Instead, he took to introducing himself as a discerning art-critic. Incapable of imparting shape to art with his palette, he could pummel art out of shape with his hands. His moustache he trained into two sharp points in the French fashion, and with equal care, sported a shaggy head of hair. He was certainly good-looking, but as he sought single-mindedly to look even better, his mirrored dressing-table groaned under the weight of a bewildering range of Parisian cosmetic products. The items on the shelf of the wash-basin alone would have more than sufficed for the ten-headed Ravana. No one dared raise a whisper about his aristocratic pedigree, since he grandly ignored expensive Havana cigars after a couple of puffs while his suits travelled all the way to France through the parcel post to be laundered every month. His sartorial measurements were registered in the kind of tailoring establishments in Europe which might easily have on their lists princely patrons of Patiala or Karpurtala. His indistinct, drawling pronunciation of the English language, liberally laced with slang, and made even more expressive with the aid of half-closed, lazy eyes, was supposed to be the very manner in which the blue-blooded English nobs hobnobbed with each other. Or so the experts said. With his additional accomplishments like the frequent use of abusive English oaths and racy bad language, he easily ruled over his set as the perfect role-model.

The full name of Katy Mitter was Ketoki. Her airs and graces were triple-distilled from her elder brother's factory of mannerisms which produced the strong, undiluted essence of English aristocracy. In proud defiance of the average Bengali girl's pride in her long hair, Katy had scissored it off. The traditional chignon had disappeared like a tadpole's tail and bore mute testimony as to how a highly evolved strain of imitation might appear to the eye. Cosmetics coated her naturally fair skin like an enamelled layer. Her black eyes, in her girlhood, had been soft; now her eyes apparently failed to register ordinary people. Even if they did so, then they failed to notice, but if they did notice, they glittered with the sharpness of a half-open blade.

Her lips had been sweet and innocent in days long gone by, but after years of smiling a sardonic, crooked smile, they had set into a permanently crooked line. I'm a novice when it comes to describing women's apparel. Its vocabulary eludes me. But I get the impression of a near-diaphanous outer cover like the slough of a snake, through which the colours from the inner clothing gleam; much of her bosom is exposed; she has perfected the art of displaying her exposed arms – sometimes on the table, sometimes on sofa handles, or lovingly entwined and lightly placed somewhere. And when she holds a cigarette between two manicured fingers tipped with long nails, it is more for ornamentation than for actually smoking. However, her penchant for high-heeled shoes certainly causes concern: it's almost as if the Creator had forgotten the model of goat-like hooves and had gravely erred in shaping the human feet as he did. The human cobblers fashioned the right evolutionary answer to improve the aesthetics of the human feet, so that the ground could be tormented at every step.

Sissy is somewhere in the middle. She hasn't quite managed to get the ultimate degree, but is certainly taking flying leaps in that direction. Her talent for inexhaustible small-talk, her high laughter and scintillating good humour give her mannerisms just the sort of lively vividness that is greatly admired by her fan-club. Our literature describes Radhika's coming-of-age as an attractive mixture of the unripe and the ripe. Sissy fits this description quite well. In her hoofed shoes the new age is victorious, but her chignon belongs to a bygone era. Her sari has climbed a couple of inches towards her ankles, but the upper limits carefully maintain the borders of feminine modesty. Her hands are unnecessarily and fashionably gloved. But both her wrists display bangles, defying the fashionable dictum of one-bangle-one-wrist. She no longer feels dizzy if she smokes, but still loves paan; pickles and mango preserves sent in biscuit tins still appeal. She prefers pitthe[84], the speciality of the Pousparban[85] to the plum puddings of Christmas. She has learned to dance from an European danseuse, but she still feels a little embarrassed to pair off and waltz on a public dance floor.

The pair came to Shillong as they felt quite perturbed at the rumours circulating about Amit. In their vocabulary, Labanya was a governess, a class created to corrupt the men in their circle. They were convinced that Labanya was a gold-digger, after money and social position, and so she had wrapped herself around Amit. To rescue Amit from her toils a female hand wielding the broom was necessary. The four-headed Brahma had not just possessed a glad eye, but had also been biased in favour of women, and so had deliberately made men thick-headed as far as these charmers were concerned. It was clearly the duty of the women of the clan, clear-headed where the wiles of their own sex were concerned, to keep their menfolk safe from the dangerous designs of unscrupulous temptresses.

---

[84] A kind of rice cake.

[85] A ritual during the month of January-February, when the harvest is reaped.

These two young women had decided on a plan of action to rescue Amit from Labanya's clutches. They had determined to say nothing to Amit at the outset but first survey the battlefield and weigh up the opposition.

They noticed immediately that Amit had acquired a film of rustic varnish. Even before this, Amit had always stood out from his own set. But, then, in those days he had been an urbane sophisticate, polished, sharp, dazzling. Now, however, he had picked up not only a healthy outdoor tan, but had been blunted a little at the touch of these green surroundings. He was behaving almost normally! Amit in his previous incarnation would duel with all subjects with the rapier of laughter, but he seemed to have completely lost all fancy for that pastime. This seemed to the two ladies fairly ominous.

Sissy actually commented on this to Amit one day, 'To us, from a distance it seemed like you were planning to turn into a Khasia. But now I see that you are getting "green", like the pine trees here – maybe this will add to your physical health – but you are no longer as interesting.'

Amit took refuge in Wordsworth and quoting him, said that nature invariably put her stamp on the body, mind and heart of anyone who chose to stay close to her – the 'mute insensate things' made their presence felt.

Sissy thought, we have no complaint towards the 'mute insensate things' but we certainly are anxious about the kind of beings who are highly conscious and are also very dextrous in the verbal art of sweet provocation.

They had hoped that Amit would raise the subject of Labanya himself. But a day went by, then two, then three — Amit remained totally silent. One thing was very evident though — Amit's life boat was being badly rocked and stood in the danger of getting capsized. Much before they even got out of their beds, Amit would be off for Destination Unknown. When he came back, his face would wear the look of a wind-whipped banana tree with tattered leaves mutely bearing witness to rough weather. Also, reliable eyes had caught sight of Robi Thakur's books in his bed, which provided still more food for concern. The inside leaf bore the name Labanya, from which the first letter had been struck off in red. Possibly the touchstone of the name had added more value to the object.

Amit was dashing out every now and then. As a pretext he would trot out, 'I'm off to work up an appetite.' Everybody had perceived the keenness of that appetite and also the source feeding it. Yet they feigned ignorance of the real cause and ostentatiously laid the reason for such a voracious appetite to the healthy air of Shillong. While Sissy laughed inwardly, Katy burned. To Amit, his own problem had assumed such gigantic proportions, he was totally incapable of observing anything extraneous to it. So he could openly tell the two friends, 'I am going to look for a waterfall.' That others could be more than a little doubtful about the nature of the 'waterfall', and its direction of descent, totally escaped his attention. Today, Amit claimed mendaciously that he would be away on an excursion — for locating honey from orange blossoms! The two girls innocently and naively declared their intention of accompanying Amit in his search for such marvellous honey, as it had whetted their curiosity. Amit cut short the discussion by saying that the way was inaccessible, completely unfit for vehicles. And ran. The two friends, observing the wayward wings of this honey-bee, decided that an immediate visit to the orange-orchard was extremely necessary. In the meantime, Noren had gone to the race-course. Though he had requested Sissy's company, she had refused. Only a deep sympathiser would be capable of divining the stern self-restraint required behind this refusal.

Chapter 15

Hindrance

The two damsels crossed the stretch of Yogamaya's garden from the main gates, but could not spot any servants. Only after they reached the portico did they see a student and her teacher at a small table on the raised porch before the house. They immediately guessed that the elder of the two was Labanya.

Katy's heels rapidly tap-tapped on the stairs and once on top, she apologised curtly, 'Sorry!'

Labanya got up from her seat and politely inquired, 'Who are you looking for?'

Katy's sharp gaze quickly swept Labanya from head to toe before she said, 'I came to know if Mr AmittRaaye is here.'

For a moment, Labanya failed to place this strange creature in the right order in the world of living things. She accordingly said, 'We don't know him.'

A lightning glance passed between the two friends, the hint of a satirical smile. Then Katy tossed her head and sharply said, 'We are aware of his visits here, oftener than is good for him.'

Labanya, sensing their hostility, suddenly and unerringly guessed their identity, and also realised she had made a bad mistake. She said uncomfortably, 'I'll get Kartama, she can give you information.'

After Labanya left, Katy asked Surama briefly, 'Your teacher?'

'Yes.'

Katy asked again, 'Is her name Labanya?'

'Yes.'

Abruptly Katy switched to English, 'Got matches?'

Unable to think of any reason why matches were suddenly necessary, Surama could not grasp the question, and stared uncomprehendingly at her interlocutor.

Katy briefly changed over to the vernacular – 'matches'.

Surama fetched a box of matches. Katy lit her cigarette and drawing on it, casually asked Surama, 'Do you study English?'

Surama managed to give an assenting little nod, and immediately retreated inside the house. Katy observed, 'Whatever else her governess may have taught her, she certainly hasn't taught her manners.'

The two friends then gave vent to a volley of comments, 'Famous Labanya! Delicious! She has turned these Shillong mountains into volcanoes! She has caused massive earthquakes that have cracked the firm terrain of Amit's heart from end to end! Silly! Men are funny!'

Sissy gave a high laugh – but there was generosity in it. Sissy had no complaints about the stupidity of men. Even she had caused an earthquake strong enough to rend a stony ground through and through! But this was extraordinarily inexplicable! On the one hand there was a girl like Katy, and on the other, that strangely-clad governess. Butter wouldn't melt in her mouth! She was so unsophisticated she resembled nothing more than a bundle of wet rags. Just sitting next to her was enough to make one's mind mouldy, like biscuits in the monsoons! How could Amit stand her for even a moment!

Said Katy with a bite, 'Sissy, your brother's mind always walks upside down! For some perverse reason, he thinks this female an angel!'

Having delivered this, Katy rested her cigarette against the algebra textbook, took out her silver-chained vanity-bag, powdered her face and, with an eye-brow pencil, touched up her eyebrows. Sissy, however, could not find it in her to blame her elder brother's whimsies – and felt indulgent instead. All her anger was directed against those sham angels who promenaded before the love-lorn gazes of men. Katy was angrily impatient of Sissy's amused dismissal of her brother's eccentricities. She felt like giving Sissy a really hard shake!

This was when Yogamaya emerged from the house in a white silk sari. Labanya was not with her. Accompanying Katy was Tabby, a tiny dog with eyes almost obscured with long hair. He had already sniffed once in the direction of Labanya and Surama to get acquainted with them. At the sight of Yogamaya the dog was suddenly seized with a brief canine infatuation. Leaping forward, he smeared her spotless attire with his muddy forepaws as a mark of his temporary affection. Sissy grabbed him by his neck and restored him to Katy. Katy tapped his nose with her forefinger and reprimanded fondly, 'Naughty dog!'

Katy did not leave her seat. She continued to smoke her cigarette while perusing that good lady with insolent indifference. Yogamaya, much more than Labanya, was the target of her fury. She was convinced that Labanya's history had a twist. To her mind, Yogamaya was masquerading as Labanya's aunt to palm her off on Amit. It did not need a great deal of intelligence to hoodwink a man – the Creator had blinkered them with his own hands!

It was Sissy who advanced and after a shadow of a greeting, said, 'I'm Sissy, Ami's sister.'

Yogamaya smiled slightly and replied, 'My dear, Ami calls me Mashima, that makes me your mashima as well.'

Having quickly taken in Katy's attitude, Yogamaya pointedly ignored her, and simply invited Sissy, 'Come, dear, come inside and sit down.'

Sissy replied, 'We don't have time, we just came to see if Ami was here.'

Yogamaya replied with equanimity, 'He hasn't come here as yet.'

Sissy asked, 'Can you tell us when he will be here?'

'I can't quite tell – well, I'll go and find out.' Yogamaya offered politely.

From her seat, Katy retorted sharply, 'That teacher sitting here, teaching, pretended never to have known Amitt!'

Yogamaya was a little confused. To her there was ample evidence of some kind of a slip-up. Equally clearly, she realised that with these young women it would be difficult to maintain her dignity, and promptly abandoned her maternal solicitude. In politely formal accents she returned, 'I have heard that Amitbabu stays with you in your hotel, I'm sure you would know his whereabouts better than I do.'

At this, Katy's deliberately pronounced smile appeared and seemed to say, 'You may hide, but you won't be able to cheat us.'

As a matter of fact, the instant Katy had set eyes on Labanya, and had heard her disclaim all knowledge of Amit, her temper had flared dangerously high. Sissy was a little worried, but her anxiety had no barbs in it. And Yogamaya's beautiful face filled with calm dignity drew her despite herself. So her mind shrank from the overt contempt which Katy displayed towards Yogamaya as she refused to rise from her seat. Yet she did not dare to take any position counter to Katy's, for Katy flattened all sedition firmly with an iron hand – she brooked no opposition to her will. Neither had she any compunction about being ruthlessly nasty. By and large people are timid, and retreat before unabashed bullying and Katy prided herself on her own harshness. She felt impatient with any erring friend who was unwise enough to betray any hint of amiability, and would unsparingly use her tongue as a cure. She flaunted her own rudeness as blunt honesty. Those who feared its lash desired to escape it at all costs, just to keep Katy in good humour. Sissy was one of them. The more nervous of Katy she felt inside, the more she imitated her to show she wasn't a weakling! But she wasn't always successful. Today Katy had immediately picked up the feeble objection that rose from a corner of Sissy's heart against her rude behaviour. She was determined to crush Sissy's incipient, unvoiced, disapproval before Yogamaya herself. She therefore rose from her seat, took a cigarette, placed it between Sissy's lips, and brought forward her own face adorned with another lit cigarette to set Sissy's alight. Sissy did not have the courage to refuse such honour. The tips of her ears turned a little red. Still, she assumed a nonchalant manner which loudly proclaimed that she was prepared to snap her fingers at the smallest frown of censure at their modern Western manners – that much for it!

Amit walked onto the scene at this moment. The damsels were totally taken aback. For somewhere in between the time he had left the hotel in a felt hat and an English shirt, he had changed into a dhoti and a shawl. His little cottage was the source of this supply. Secreted away in that nook was a book shelf, a chest of clothes and Yogamaya's gift, an armchair. He sought refuge there after having lunch in the hotel. Labanya had tightened up the rules these days, and nobody was allowed in during the time she taught Surama, whether in search of waterfalls or for orange-blossom honey. Amit had no polite reason for gaining entry into the house to slake either his intellectual or physical thirst before tea-time, fixed at four thirty in the afternoon. He would somehow while away this time before rushing here at the appointed hour, with suitable clothes on.

Today the ring had arrived from Calcutta before he had left the hotel. He had imagined exactly how ceremoniously he would put the ring on Labanya's finger. Today was a special day. This day could not be kept waiting at the gates and all work should be shelved in its honour. He had chalked out a plan of action — he would go right up to the spot where Labanya was engaged with Surama and announce — the Badshah, mounted on an elephant, had come to his newly-constructed palace — but the arch was low, and the Badshah did not want to bow his proud head and so had turned back without entering his new abode. One of our grandest days has arrived — but on the size of the arch of your leisure hours you've been miserly — break it — let the king enter with his head held high.

Amit had also thought of yet another pronouncement that he would make to her — to arrive at the right time is called punctuality. Clock time is not quite time, for it counts out the numerals mechanically, but remains ignorant of their value.

Amit then glanced outside and saw that the sky was heavily overcast — the dim daylight indicated late afternoon — at least five or six. Like a relieved mother, observing that her long-ailing son's fever had broken, would not check it with a thermometer, Amit ignored his watch, in case it gave the vulgar lie to the sky's statement. Today Amit had arrived much before the appointed time. For high hope is shameless.

The corner of the verandah that Labanya usually occupied while teaching her student was clearly visible from the road. He saw that the place was empty today. His heart leapt up in joy. Only now he glanced at his watch, to find it still saying it was twenty minutes after three. Just the other day he had told Labanya, humans were bound by discipline, but indiscipline belonged to the gods; we practice hard discipline in this world just in the hope of getting the right to taste the nectar of indiscipline in heaven. We occasionally catch a glimpse of that heaven on this earth, and we have to salute it by duly breaking discipline. He had a wild hope that maybe the glory of indiscipline had finally burst upon Labanya. Had the special day touched her all unknown, and snapped the disciplinary shackles of ordinary days?

He came closer and saw Yogamaya standing stunned before her own door, and Sissy lighting the cigarette protruding from her lips from Katy's cigarette. He had no difficulty in comprehending this as a deliberate insult. The dog, Tabby, had been curbed in his first rush of friendliness, and had curled himself up for sleep at Katy's feet. He again grew unruly at Amit's approach and began to bark and prance in a rousing welcome. Sissy again demonstrated through stern action that such ill-placed methods for expressing fondness would not be appreciated at all.

Amit did not even glance at the two companions. He called out 'Mashi' even while he was still at some distance, and coming up, he prostrated himself before her in a deep obeisance. He normally did not do so. He then asked, 'Where is Labanya?'

'I don't quite know, Baba, somewhere inside, I suppose,' Yogamaya replied.

Amit observed, 'There is still time left over from her teaching schedule.'

Yogamaya answered, 'Most probably she called it a day and went inside after these visitors arrived.'

'Come, let's see what she's up to.' Amit escorted Yogamaya back inside the house, without even deigning to acknowledge any other living presence before him.

Sissy raised her voice considerably to deliver her impression of this behaviour, 'An Insult! Come Katy, let's go!'

Katy was no less stung. But she did not want to leave without seeing the matter through to the bitter end.

'It won't have any result.' Sissy was fatalistic.

'There has to be some result.' Katy was emphatic – and her large eyes grew even larger with the strength of her feelings.

Some more time passed by. Sissy again said, a touch pleadingly, 'Bhai[86], let's go, I don't want to stay here any more.'

But Katy refused to budge from the verandah. She only said, 'He'll have to come out some time from this door.'

At long last Amit emerged, with Labanya at his side. Labanya's face wore an expression of gentle peace – no trace of rage, insolence or resentment showed on it. Yogamaya was

---

[86]Brother, a corruption of Bhrātā (Sanskrit). But it is used in a gender-neutral way even by women.

trying to remain indoors, she had no desire to come out again. But Amit was adamant, and would not allow her to retreat from the scene. Katy noticed the ring on Labanya's finger instantly. The blood rushed to her head, her eyes reddened, she felt like kicking the world.

Amit said, 'Mashi, this is my sister Shamita. My father had perhaps thought of a name that should have rhymed with mine, but they remained delinked. This is Ketoki, my sister's friend.

In the meantime, yet another uproar ensued. Surama's pet cat had strolled out, and true to his canine ethics, Tabby declared war on such daring. He would first advance to hurl aggressive challenges at the feline member. But doubtful of the outcome of an open battle, for the cat bared its claws and hissed, Tabby would retreat ignominiously. He finally concluded that non-violent scolding from a safe distance would be the wisest course to follow, and let loose a veritable volley of barks. The cat merely arched its back and turned away, obviously considering any retaliation beneath its dignity. Katy's patience snapped at this point. Highly infuriated, she began pinching the dog's ear. A lot of this violence was actually directed at herself. The dog announced its opinion of such discourtesy in a series of shrill yelps. And Fate smiled soundlessly.

When this pandemonium had abated somewhat, Amit turned to Sissy and said pointedly, 'Sissy, this lady's name is Labanya. You have never heard me utter her name, but that you've heard it from ten different sources is pretty apparent. Our marriage has been fixed for this coming *aghran*, in Calcutta.

Katy immediately pinned a smile to her face and said, 'I congratulate you. Obviously orange-blossom honey wasn't so terribly hard to get. The path wasn't inaccessible either, and anyway, the honey itself invitingly leapt forward, close to the lips!'

Sissy, as was her wont, giggled.

Labanya was aware of a malicious innuendo, but the jibe eluded her.

Amit explained to her, 'As I was leaving this morning, these girls had asked me where I was off to. I had answered, in search of honey. So they are laughing now. It's completely my fault. People just can't understand when I seriously mean what I say.'

Katy said quite quietly, 'You have won your orange-blossom honey, but now you must also ensure that I don't lose out here.'

Amit readily answered, 'Tell me what I can do.'

Katy was fairly composed in her response, 'I had a bet with Noren. He had thrown at me a challenge — that you'll never be found at *the* gentlemen's haunt — you'll never ever go to the races. I had staked this diamond ring of mine on my ability to take you to the races. Since then, I've been chasing a shadow at all the waterfalls, all the honey shops, and finally I've run you to ground here. Do bear me out Sissy — haven't I been on a long pursuit — what the English call a wild-goose chase?'

Sissy merely laughed.

Katy continued in the same vein, 'A story comes to mind — and this story I've got from you, Amitt! Some Persian philosopher, unable to track down the thief who had filched his turban, finally settled down to wait in the graveyard. His logic was simple – the thief would, at some point, have to come to the graveyard. I own I became confused when Miss Labanya here said she didn't know Amitt, but my mind knew that Amitt would surely come to this graveyard of his!'

Sissy shouted with laughter.

Now Katy addressed Labanya, 'Amitt did not utter your name, but in honeyed metaphors he spoke of orange-blossom honey! You are too naïve, you don't have such a cunning way with words, and so you blurted out that you didn't even know Amitt! The Sunday school maxims have failed completely – for neither of you received any punishment! To crown it all, one managed to empty the inaccessible orange-blossom nectar in one drought, the other managed to immediately recognise an unknown stranger at a glance – and only I stand to lose here? Sissy, don't you think this is really unfair?'

Another burst of high laughter from Sissy. In this general hilarity, Tabby thought it was his duty to join in – and duly showed signs of participation. For the third time he was ruthlessly repressed.

Katy was still composed, but emotion was creeping in now, 'Amitt, you know very well if I lose this diamond ring, the world will hold no further comfort for me. You had once given it to me. I have never taken it off for a moment, it has become a part of me. Now among these hills of Shillong, a rash bet will take it off my finger!'

Sissy could not help asking, 'Bhai, why bet at all?'

Katy returned, 'I had an unshakable pride in myself, and total faith and trust in someone else. My pride is broken, my race is run, I've lost! I don't think I'll be able to persuade Amitt to come to the races any more. But if you had thought of winning with such a trump card, why did you give me this ring so lovingly? Were there no bonds in that giving? Didn't it imply that you would shield me from all insults, always?'

As she spoke, Katy's voice grew heavy with tears, but she struggled to keep them back.

It was all of seven years ago, Katy was just eighteen. That day Amit had taken this ring off his own finger and put it on hers. This was when they were both in England. A young Punjabi lad at Oxford had been infatuated with Katy. He and Amit had had a friendly rowing match on the river, and Amit had won. The June sky, flooded with moon-light, seemed about to speak, the earth seemed to have gone insane in its rush to push up flowers in great profusion and a staggering range of colours in the rolling meadows. Amit had chosen this moment to put the ring on Katy's finger. In this act, much was left unsaid, but the unspoken words were no secret. Katy's face had not then acquired its patina of paint, her smile was sweet, strong emotions could still make her blush. Once the ring had changed fingers, Amit had softly whispered in her ear,

> *'Tender is the night*
> *And haply the queen moon is on her throne.'*

The Katy of those days was untutored in small talk. She could only murmur half to herself on a great sigh, '*mon ami*', which in French meant 'My dearest!'

Today, Amit too, groped for an answer. A quick reply evaded him.

Katy's hard-won control over her feelings was slipping as she went on, 'If I've lost the bet, let this everlasting symbol of my defeat remain with you, Amitt. I won't allow it to tell a lie on my finger.'

And Katy, taking off the ring from her finger, put it on the table, and hurried away, with tears streaming down her enamelled face.

Chapter 16

Freedom

*L*abanya received a small letter, written in Shobhanlal's hand:

I arrived in Shillong last night. If you grant me permission to visit you, I will do so. If you don't, I'll leave tomorrow. My punishment at your hands has been very real. But even today I am puzzled as to when and how I erred. I have come today to hear your reasons from you, till then my soul cannot rest in peace. Don't be apprehensive. I have no other prayer.

Labanya's eyes filled with tears. She wiped them away. And she stilled deep within herself, turned and stared back at her own past contemplatively. She remembered with deep compassion the timidity of the little seedling that might have grown, and yet which had been denied sustenance, and been blighted in its early spring. Perhaps, had he taken over her life then, meaning and fulfilment would have been infused in it. But in those days she had been aggressively independent, filled with the pride of knowledge, and had single-mindedly pursued it. In her father's new-found love she had perceived only weakness and had mentally condemned it. Today love had taken its revenge, and her hauteur was ground to dust. What might have been as easy as breath, as simple as innocent laughter, had become difficult. She felt diffident about welcoming the guest of yesterday with open arms, and yet the thought of turning him away pierced her heart. The memory of Shobhanlal's hurt, hesitating face flashed into her memory. So much time had elapsed, yet on what divine nectar did that young man's rejected love survive the long cruel draught? In its own intrinsic greatness.

Labanya wrote in the letter:

Of all my friends, you are the noblest. Today I don't have the wealth which would fully pay for such friendship. You have never asked for payment. True to yourself, even today you have come to give whatever is yours to give, without making any demands. I have no longer the strength or the pride to return it saying I don't need it.

She had written the letter and had sent it off when Amit came and said, 'Bonya, let's go for a walk today.'

Amit had suggested this nervously, for he had thought Labanya would refuse his request. But Labanya acquiesced easily. 'Let's go', she said.

They left. Very hesitantly Amit tried to take Labanya's hand within his. Labanya did not resist at all, but allowed Amit to hold it. Amit grasped it strongly, hoping his grip would convey his feelings as he had completely run out of words! They halted at the same spot where the mountains and the forest had suddenly drawn back slightly, leaving a little clearing. The sun touched a bare mountain top with its last ray and sank down. A wonderful green softly shaded, and then faded into a gentle blue. The two stood quietly, facing this colour-play.

Labanya asked very gently then, 'Why did you take off a ring today which you had placed on someone's finger at some point, and that too, through me?'

Amit, deeply pained, answered, 'Bonya, I don't know how to explain everything to you. I had placed the ring on a totally different girl from the one who took it off today – they are not the same person.'

'One of them the Creator had created with love, the other is the product of your indifference,' Labanya replied wisely.

'That is not totally correct. Today's Katy is not the result of the pressure of my neglect alone,' defended Amit.

Labanya said gravely and calmly, 'Maybe not, Mita. But why didn't you nurture as your very own someone who had delivered herself completely in your hands? For whatever reason, first your hold on her had loosened, and then ten other influences got to work on her and she changed. It was because she had lost your regard in the first place that she thought to win the favour of ten other people by transforming herself! Today she is like a doll in a foreign shop! Had her heart been still alive, that wouldn't have been possible. Never mind – let it go! I have a request. You have to grant it.'

Amit answered, 'Of course, just say it.'

Labanya said, 'For at least a week go to Cherrapunji for a holiday with your friends. Even if you cannot make her happy, you can at least give her some entertainment.'

Amit remained quiet for a while and then assented reluctantly, 'Very well.'

Then Labanya laid her head on Amit's breast and gently said, 'Let me tell you something, Mita, I'll never say it again. You don't have to bear any responsibility for this deep emotional tie between us. With all the strength of my love, untouched by any anger, I say, don't give me this ring, there's no need for such external symbols. Let my love be unadorned, unshadowed by anything extrinsic to it.'

With that, Labanya took off the ring and gently slid it on Amit's finger. Amit did not resist.

Like the earth, bathed in the twilight, offering its face to the glowing sky, Labanya lifted her face lit in just such a quiet, calm way towards Amit's face.

Amit was back almost before the mandatory seven days were up and immediately headed for Yogamaya's house. The house was shut, everybody had gone. They had left no forwarding address.

Amit came and stood under that eucalyptus tree, his mind blank, and then aimlessly wandered about. The familiar gardener came up and asked him, 'Babu, shall I open up the house? Will you sit inside?' Amit hesitated a little and then said, 'Yes.'

Once inside, he made straight for Labanya's living-room. The chair, table and the shelf – were all there, the books were gone. A couple of torn empty envelopes lay on the floor, with Labanya's name and address written on them in an unknown hand. On the table were scattered some discarded quills and a tiny pencil stub. Amit pocketed the pencil. The next room was the bedroom. On the iron bedstead there was a single mattress, and on the mirrored dressing table an empty bottle of hair oil. Amit stretched out on the bed with his head clasped between his hands, the bed squeaked under his weight. The room bore a mute, desolate air. It could say nothing to any question put to it. It had swooned, from which it could never be roused.

His body and mind weighted down with an enormous listlessness, Amit went to his own cottage. It was exactly the way he had left it. Even the arm-chair Yogamaya had left untouched. He knew she had left it for him out of sheer affection, and once again her calm and sweet tones sounded in his ears – 'Baba!' Amit prostrated himself in front of the armchair in homage.

All the beauty of the Shillong mountains had fled. There was no solace for Amit anywhere.

Chapter 17

The Final Ode

*J*yotishankar was studying in a college in Calcutta. He lived in the hostel attached to the Presidency College in Kolutala. Amit often brought him home, fed him up, read books with him, frequently startled him with his unique comments, and took him for spins in his motor-car.

Then for a while Jyotishankar did not get any definite news of Amit. Now he heard he was in Nainital, then again perhaps he was in Ootacamund. One day he heard a friend of Amit mockingly remark that Amit was very busy in scrubbing off Katy Mitter's many-hued, glittery exterior. It was a task much to his liking – effecting total transformations. So long Amit had worked with words to sculpt images, now he had a real, live human being. That being was also very willing to shed her colourful petals, hoping that the ultimate metamorphosis would bear the much-desired fruit. Amit's sister, Lissy, had been heard saying that Katy was almost unrecognisable, so very natural did she look. She had even instructed her friends to call her Ketoki. For Katy this was certainly shameless behaviour, like a really bashful girl inexplicably switching from her usual attire of transparent Shantipuri[87] sarees to heavy jackets and voluminous underclothes! Amit apparently had taken to calling her 'Keya' in private. People had also been whispering about their supposed boating expedition in Nainital, where Katy had been at the boat's helm, while Amit had read out Robi Thakur's *A Voyage for the Unknown* to her. But people say so many things. Jyotishankar merely gathered from all this that Amit's mind had fled to his theory of holidays – and was swimming there mid-stream!

Finally Amit returned. The news of his impending marriage with Ketaki had spread all over town. Yet Jyoti hadn't heard a word of all this from Amit himself. Amit's own behaviour had changed. Though he still presented him with English books, he did not spend his evenings discussing them with him. Jyoti understood that the course of these discussions had veered towards a new abyss. Nowadays he did not call Jyoti out for car-rides. Jyoti was precisely at the age when he could intuitively

---

[87] Shantipur is a small town in Bengal which specialised in the weaving of extra-fine cotton cloth. A sari or dhoti from Shantipur was normally prefaced with the term 'Shantipuri'.

divine that Amit's party, setting out on 'A Voyage for the Unknown', would not admit a third member.

Finally, Jyoti could not curb his curiosity and asked Amit directly, 'Amitda, I heard you are getting married to Miss Ketoki Mitra?'

Amit was silent for a while and then he asked, 'Does Labanya know of this?'

'No, I haven't written to her. I hadn't heard you confirm it, so I kept quiet,' Jyoti said.

'It's true, but perhaps Labanya will misunderstand.'

This time Jyoti grinned, 'Where's the space for misunderstanding here? If you are getting married, you are – plain and simple.'

'Look Jyoti, nothing is plain and simple where human beings are concerned. The dictionary fixes a meaning, but as it interacts with a human variable, the meaning splits in seven different ways, like the Ganga branching off as it nears the sea.' Amit performed a verbal sleight of hand which left his devoted disciple far behind.

Jyoti said gropingly, 'You mean to say that marriage does not mean marriage?'

Amit expanded his cryptic statement a little more, 'I'm saying that marriage has a thousand meanings – which blends with different human variables to acquire specific meanings. It is perplexing to try and fix its meaning without the human element.'

'Why don't you give me your specific meaning,' Jyoti besought Amit, keen to dispel the intellectual fog around this word.

'I cannot define it, explanations will have to come from life. If I say its root word is love, then I go off at a tangent into another word. Because love is even more dynamic than marriage, as far as words and their meanings go.' Amit was still maddeningly elusive, much to his disciple's dismay.

'Then Amitda, we have to stop speaking altogether! If we have to heft a word across our shoulders and chase the meaning, while the meaning dodges left and right as we run after it in hot pursuit, all communication will just stop!' Jyoti was pardonably exasperated.

Amit became the patronising older man approving of a promising youngster, 'That's not bad, brother! In my company you've picked up verbal skills. Communication must somehow go on, and so words are necessary. Some words we deliberately clip when we pull them into market-use, for the reality they contain cannot be expressed in words – so the words remain, but shorn of meaning. Nothing to be done! We just shut our eyes and somehow get on with communication.'

Jyoti was palpably dissatisfied, 'Then must one simply drop the word that came up today?'

Amit continued to hover out of Jyoti's range, 'If the discussion is for some intellectual curiosity, no harm in dropping it, but if it's a craving of the heart, conditions become different.'

Jyoti said, 'Suppose it's a craving of the heart.'

Amit finally relented, 'Bravo! Then listen.'

Here a little footnote would not be amiss. Jyoti nowadays is a regular at Amit's youngest sister Lissy's tea-table. He has become addicted to the cup of tea personally poured out by her. It can be therefore safely surmised that Jyoti has no hard feelings about Amit's secession from the regular literary discussions and the motor-rides in the evening. He has forgiven him wholeheartedly.

Amit began, 'Oxygen is invisible but present in the air, without which we can't breathe. Then again, oxygen combines with coal for combustion – and fire has many uses – neither of these two functions can be left out. Have you understood now?'

Jyoti persevered, 'Not completely, but I'm willing to be instructed.'

Amit stated, 'The love that freely pervades the sky is the mate of our inner self; the everyday love which is ever-present in our daily lives is the help-mate. I want both.'

Jyoti was still floundering out of his depth and said a shade helplessly, 'I can't quite make out if I'm receiving your meaning clearly. Be a bit more explicit, Amitda.'

Amit said, 'One day I had spread out my wings and had sailed through the skies. Today, I've found my nest, and am sitting with my wings furled. But there is still the sky.'

Jyoti asked, 'But can't marriage combine both the mate and the help-mate in one figure?'

Amit answered, 'Many probable opportunities exist in life but they may never actually come. Lucky is he who gets half the kingdom and the princess in a matching set! But the fellow who fortunately manages a kingdom from somewhere and a princess from somewhere else, is fairly lucky too.'

Jyoti was doubtful, 'But —'

Amit perceived what was troubling Jyoti, 'Ah, you think what you call romance will be missing from this cocktail. Not at all! Romance shouldn't be rationed out in limited quantities and dished out in the moulds provided by fiction! Certainly not! I'll create my own romance. My heavens will hold romance, my earthly existence will also hold romance! You call only those romantic who, in futile efforts to save one, completely impoverishes the other! Either they swim like fish in water, or they prowl on the land like cats, or fly like bats in the sky. I'm the paramahansa[88] of romance. Being single-minded, I'll only employ my strength to understand the truth of love — in water, on land or in the skies. I'll be at home on terra firma, and when I'm winging to an idea, I'll take the open routes of the skies. Victory to my Labanya, victory to my Ketaki, and glory to Amit Rai under all conditions!'

Jyoti sat in stunned silence, such views made him uncomfortable. Amit, realising his discomfort, smiled a little and said, 'Look, brother, meanings are not the same for everyone. Perhaps what I'm saying is just my perception. If I try to understand this as your meaning too, you'll misunderstand me and roundly abuse me. In this world, riots and bloodshed occur because one person's meaning is thrust on someone else's words. Let me tell you my own meaning with the help of analogies — words used directly become too blunt, then they

---

[88] Paramahansa or swan, who can use its beak to filter slime and glean food.

grow ashamed of the weight they carry! My relation to Ketaki is definitely love – but it's like water in a pitcher – for everyday use. And my love for Labanya is like a lake, it cannot be brought home, my mind will swim there in abandon.'

Jyoti was doubtful, 'But Amitda, shouldn't one choose between the two?'

Amit shrugged away the question, 'If one can, sure, but I cannot.'

Jyoti could not lay aside his doubts so easily, 'But if Shrimati Ketaki –'

Amit said briefly, 'She knows. I can't say if she understands completely. I'll try to explain to her throughout the rest of my life that I am not cheating her. She also has to understand that she is indebted to Labanya.'

Jyoti gave it up and said, 'Whatever it may be, the news of your engagement has to be given to Shrimati Labanya.'

Amit replied, 'Yes, of course. But first I want to give her a letter, will you deliver it to her?'

Jyoti answered, 'Sure.'

This was Amit's letter:

That evening, when we stood at the end of a chapter, a journey, we ended it with poetry. Today, too, I have halted at the end of another road. On this last moment I want to leave a poetic note. It won't be able to bear anything heavier than that. The wretched Nibaran Chakraborty died as soon as he was found out – like the most delicate fish. So I turn to your poet for my last words to you, no help for it.

In your very absence I behold your immortal form.
Your final advent, unseen, in the concealed chambers of my heart.
The eternal touchstone I suddenly hold in my grasp.
You freely filled my emptiness with noble generosity.

In the very moment when I despaired in the gloom,
I discovered the steadily burning flame of the evening lamp,
In the inner temple of my being.
From the sacrificial fires of separation,
Emerged Love in the gentle glow of sorrow as reverent homage.

Mita

Some more time flowed by. That day Ketoki had gone to attend her sister's daughter's annaprasan[89]. Amit had stayed behind. He was sprawling in an armchair, his legs resting on the seat before him, reading the letters of William James, when Jyoti came in and gave him Labanya's letter. The first page of the letter bore the news of Labanya's engagement to Shobhanlal. The marriage was to take place six months later, on the summit of Ramgarh mountain, in May. The other page had a poem:

---

[89] Annaprasan is the ritual celebration of the first solid food given to a baby (normally at six months).

SESHER KOBITA – THE LAST POEM

Hark at the clamour of time on its unending journey.
Its invisible chariot pounds through our hearts in frenetic beat.
Crushed under its trundling wheels, in the universal void,
The exploded stars do weep.
O dearest friend, the same relentless time
Has netted me in its coils
And now bears me swiftly away
In its chariot,
On a new, reckless journey,
Far, very far away from you.
Leaping over a thousand deaths,
Or so it seems to me,
On a new peak now stand I,
Touched by the fingers of a new dawn.
Whirling my old name has gone,
In the chariot's furious wake.
There never can be any turning back.
Even if you glimpse me from afar,
Your glance will slide away, as off a stranger.
O, my friend, farewell.

On a leisure-filled, lazy day,
As spring steps briskly in the air,
When winds blow from the shores of the
past in a gentle sigh,
And the gentle tears of the fallen bakul fills the sky,

A bit of me still, that moment will yield,
Till then tucked in some niche of your heart.
A dull, forgetful morning it will perhaps set alight,
And may even transform into some nameless dream.
Yet, no, not a dream.
It is the conqueror of Death,
My deepest truth, it is my Love.
Unchanging, true, this offering of mine
For you I have left behind.
But I, caught up in this web of time,
Am swept away
On the swift current of change.
O, my friend, farewell.

You have suffered no harm.
Though my make is but of mortal clay,
Yet a divine presence you've wrought in your heart.
Your playful homage to her in the soft half twilight,
Will remain unmarred by the mortal, the ordinary touch,
That my every-day self will bring.
Your perfect offering in aesthetic settings,
Will not be damaged by paroxysms of emotional thirst.
Your feast of the mind, which you lovingly displayed
With the craving of creativity,
I will not soil
With my earthly wants, or dampen with my tears.
Perhaps you will create still,

From the shards of my memory, another dream,
But with no burdensome responsibility,
With no irksome weight.
O dearest friend, farewell.

Don't be sad for me.
I've work, I hold in my hand the whole world.
My bowl is not empty.
My vow is the constant refilling of lack.
If someone suffers enough to wait,
Anxious and vigilant,
He bestows on me the most blessed state.
He, who, on a dark, moonless night, proffer,
The pure white rajanigandh[90] culled from the full-moon
bright,
He does accept me,
Good and bad together, as I am,
With limitless compassion.
To him do I offer up this life.
You have the everlasting right
Over whatever little I gave as a gift.
Here, I give of myself, bit by bit.
The tender moments that I offer up from my heart,
He drains to the very dregs.

---

[90] Rajanigandhā (The perfume of the night) or tube-roses.

THE FINAL ODE

You are glorious in your limitless wealth,
O, peerless one!
I have merely returned what you yourself generously gave,
The more you accepted, the more indebted I became.
O dearest friend, farewell.

Bonya

Select Bibliography

Davis, Con and Schleifer, Ronald, 1991. *Criticism & Culture: The Role of Critique in Modern Literary Theory*, Longman, London.

Derrida, Jacques, 1978. Alan Bass (tr.), *Writing and Difference*. Routledge, London.

Derek Attridge (ed.), 1992. *Acts of Literature*, Routledge, London, New York.

Doniger, Wendy, & Smith, Brian K. 1991.*The Laws of Manu*. Penguin, New Delhi.

Dowson, John, (1973). *A Classical Dictionary of Hindu Mythology and Religion, Geography, History and Literature*. Navchetan Press, Delhi.

Dutta, Krishna & Robinson, Andrew, (1997), 2000. *Rabindranath Tagore: The Myriad-minded Man*, Rupa, New Delhi.

Ions, Veronica, (1967), 1992. *Indian Mythology*, Prakash Books, New Delhi.

Leitch, Vincent, B, Cain, William E, Finke, Laurie, Johnson, Barbara, (eds). 2001. *The Norton Anthology of Theory and Criticism*, Norton, London, New York.

Mani, Vettam, (1969, 1975, 1979) 1984. *Puranic Encyclopaedia: A Comparitive Dictionary of Special Reference to the Epic and Puranic Literature*. Motilal Banarsidass. Delhi.

Matchett, Freda, 'The Puranas', Gavin Flood (ed.). 2003. *The Blackwell Companion to Hinduism*, Blackwell, Oxford.

Radice, William, 2003. *Poetry and Community, Lectures and Essays (1991-2001)*, Chronicle Books, New Delhi.

Scholes, Robert, Comley, Nancy R., Klauss, Carl H., Silverman, Michael. (1978, 1982, 1986, 1991) 1999. *Elements of Literature: Essay, Drama, Film, Poetry, Fiction*. Oxford University Press, Delhi.

Sen, Sukumar.(1996) 1998. *Bangla Sahityer Itihaas (The History of Bengali Literature), Rabindranath Thakur*, 4, Ananda Publishers Private Ltd. Calcutta.

———, 1999. *Bangla Sahityer Itihaas (The History of Bengali Literature), 1891-1941*, 5, Ananda Publishers Private Ltd. Calcutta.

Tagore, Rabindranath, *Farewell My Friend and The Garden*,Kripalani, Krishna (tr.), (1999) 2000. Jaico Publishing House, Mumbai.

——— 'Ghare Bairey', *Rabindra Rachanabali*, (1402 BS) 1995. 4, Sulabh Sanskaran, 125th Centenary Celebrations, Vishvabharati, Kolkata. p.469 ff.

——— 'Yogayog', *Rabindra Rachanabali*, (1402 BS) 1995. 5, Sulabh Sanskaran, 125th Centenary Celebrations, Vishvabharati, Kolkata, p.321 ff.

―――― 'Sesher Kobita', *Rabindra Rachanabali*, (1402 BS) 1995. 5, Sulabh Sanskaran, 125th Centenary Celebrations, Vishvabharati, Kolkata, p.457 ff.

―――― 'Chaar Adhyay', *Rabindra Rachanabali*, (1402 BS) 1995. 7, Sulabh Sanskaran, 125th Centenary Celebrations, Vishvabharati, Kolkata, p.457 ff.

Worton, Michael and Still, Judith, (1990), 1991. *Intertextuality: Theories and Practices*. Manchester University Press, Manchester, New York.